There was no way she was going to be the only one naked here...

Anne reached for Blake, pulling him into the shower. "I want you," she whispered.

"I'm fully clothed."

"I don't care." She grabbed the hem of his shirt, pulling the soaked cotton up his body and over his head in one smooth motion.

Blake's eyes glazed as her hot, wet skin touched his own. He leaned down to her shoulder to lap at a trail of water droplets, following it to the swell of her breast.

Anne whimpered as he studiously ignored the aching point waiting for him.

Finally, he flicked his tongue out, taking the tiniest taste of her. She gasped, her knees buckling and her body sagging. His arms tightened around her and he reached down to lift her legs and wrap them tight around his waist.

She moved against him, reaching up with her mouth to claim his lips, urging him on to what they both wanted.

Blaze™

Dear Reader,

The moment Anne Sobel stepped onto the page in *Whispers in the Dark* I knew there was more to her than met the eye. She was hiding something and I was determined to learn what her secret was. However, the more I got to know her the more my determination morphed into a need to find this wonderfully different and sad woman the perfect person to share her life with.

It didn't take me long to realize that Blake Mitchell was an ideal fit. A man struggling with demons of his own, not only would he understand her drive for independence, he'd protect her with his life—whether she wanted him to or not.

I hope you enjoy reading about Anne and Blake's journey. I'd love to hear what you think of their story! You can contact me at kira@kirasinclair.com or visit me at www.KiraSinclair.com.

Best Wishes,

Kira

Kira Sinclair

CAUGHT OFF GUARD

HARLEQUIN®

TORONTO • NEW YORK • LONDON
AMSTERDAM • PARIS • SYDNEY • HAMBURG
STOCKHOLM • ATHENS • TOKYO • MILAN • MADRID
PRAGUE • WARSAW • BUDAPEST • AUCKLAND

Recycling programs
for this product may
not exist in your area.

ISBN-13: 978-0-373-79592-5

CAUGHT OFF GUARD

ABOUT THE AUTHOR

When not working as an office manager for a project management firm or juggling plotlines, Kira spends her time on a small farm in North Alabama with her wonderful husband, two amazing daughters and a menagerie of animals. It's amazing to see how this self-proclaimed city girl has (or has not, depending on who you ask) adapted to country life. Kira enjoys hearing from her readers at www.KiraSinclair.com. Or stop by www.writingplayground.blogspot.com and join in the fight to stop the acquisition of an alpaca.

Books by Kira Sinclair
HARLEQUIN BLAZE
415—WHISPERS IN THE DARK
469—AFTERBURN

Don't miss any of our special offers. Write to us at the following address for information on our newest releases.

Harlequin Reader Service
U.S.: 3010 Walden Ave., P.O. Box 1325, Buffalo, NY 14269
Canadian: P.O. Box 609, Fort Erie, Ont. L2A 5X3

Anne and Karyn share a bond that I can write only because of my relationship with my sister. Thank you, Beth, for showing me what love, understanding and friendship are all about. Love ya!

I want to thank Lynn Raye Harris and her husband, Mike, who assisted me with my military information. Any mistakes are solely my own.

1

SOMEONE WAS WATCHING HER. Again.

The sensation was…familiar. Annemarie Sobel Prescott might not have experienced it for a while but the muscles at the back of her neck still bunched in memory.

This was different though. The awareness of his gaze didn't make her feel dirty and exposed. The man staring at her from across the crowded ballroom didn't have dollar signs in his eyes and an intrusive camera lens trained on her every sin. Nope, Blake Mitchell had lust and appreciation in his eyes.

She liked that infinitely better.

From the moment she'd grown breasts the paparazzi had been her constant companion. Other kids inherited red hair or a talent for singing. She'd inherited the world's interest in every aspect of her life. Her entire misspent youth had been caught on camera. Sex, drugs and mischief had been her hobbies—and she'd been damn good at all three. Headlines had been her specialty.

Hotel Heiress Caught in Torrid Affair with Married Hollywood Heartthrob.

At least until she'd walked away from it all.

She glanced across the room at him again. She couldn't help herself, the weight of his eyes on her was too much to ignore. He was in a dark corner, one shoulder tight against the wall, running his fingers languidly up and down the side of a tumbler full of ice and amber liquid. She could see the beads of condensation as he absently spread them against the glass.

An image of those fingers stroking her skin instead flashed through her mind. Her body melted, a slow burning heat settling into the pit of her belly.

He pushed away from the wall, taking two steps toward her. The coward in her wanted to bolt. The intensity she could see churning in his eyes scared and thrilled her at the same time.

He took a step forward; she took a step back, right into yards of silk.

"Thank you. Thank you. Thank you."

Her best friend, Karyn Mitchell...no, it was Karyn Faulkner now, grabbed her around the waist and crushed her against the flowing silk of her white wedding gown.

Anne hugged her friend back, letting her eyes stray for just a second to gauge Blake's progress. He'd stopped, probably brought up quick at the sight of his sister giving her a bear hug.

A sigh of relief—and regret—escaped silently through her lips before she returned her focus to her friend. "You're welcome, but I didn't do anything."

Pulling back, Karyn eyed her. "Don't you lie to me. I know just what it cost you to get this place."

Anne fought to keep a twist of distaste from forming on her lips. "So I called in a favor." At least it hadn't required that she actually speak to her mother, although she was certain the senior manager of the Darby, Mississippi, Prescott Hotel had wasted no time in telling the CEO about the last-minute accommodation. Anne probably should have warned the woman that the favor wouldn't gain her any brownie points with her mother…. But then they might not have gotten the room.

While she, Karyn and Chris lived in Birmingham, the rest of Karyn's family was still in Mississippi. And Karyn had her heart set on getting married in her hometown of Darby, surrounded by family. Unfortunately, no venues had been available.

Anne would do anything if it meant making Karyn happy, even call on the family name she'd abandoned.

Chris slipped up beside them, curling his hand around Karyn's waist. It was an absent gesture of familiarity that made envy bloom in the center of Anne's chest.

"Enjoy yourself! Dance. Drink. Be merry. Chris's cousin seems nice." Karyn's eyebrows waggled up and down and a smile lit her face. She was so different now that she'd found Chris, more open.

"Actually, I suggest you stay away from Adam." Chris mimed a glass to his lips and shook his head before leaning down to whisper something in Karyn's ear. She looked up at her new husband with love and devotion and placed a kiss to the underside of his jaw.

Anne watched them walk away. Chris pulled Karyn into his arms. They could have been alone in the room crowded with laughing, chattering people. They only had eyes for each other.

Loneliness mixed with the envy.

She was happy for her friend. Honestly, she was. But at the same time she recognized things in her world would change. Had already changed.

Once again, she was alone.

She glanced away from the lovebirds, feeling as if she was invading their privacy. Her eyes unerringly found their way back to Blake.

He moved from the dark shadows surrounding the dance floor, almost as if he'd been waiting for her. All around her couples danced, laughed, touched…kissed. Candlelight was everywhere.

Tongues of light flickered across Blake as he walked toward her. A slash of brightness across the dark planes of his face. A flash of orange-red against the black of his tux. The shadows played, revealing, highlighting and then hiding again. But the fire that flickered in his eyes never wavered.

It didn't take a genius to figure out he was heading for her. It also didn't take a genius to know exactly what he wanted. The burning sensation low in her belly told her she wanted the same thing.

That didn't mean she was going to get it. Or take it. Or…whatever.

Karyn had told her all about Blake, the middle child and her older brother. They'd talked about his relentless need to shoulder responsibility for things that weren't his to bear—like the fact that he'd introduced his sister to the man who had raped her, and couldn't seem to forgive himself.

In Anne's other world, the one where she'd done, said and demanded anything she'd wanted, Blake being her best friend's brother wouldn't have mattered. Now, somehow it did. She didn't want to use him simply because loneliness was crowding in tonight.

However, she wasn't sure she'd be able to do the right thing. Not when his eyes burned as they traveled the length of her body. A shiver of anticipation passed slowly down her spine.

He weaved in and out of people, as if the crowd between them didn't exist. In seconds he stood before her, a smile playing at the edges of his lips. "May I?"

It had been a long time since she'd been tempted to sin. Staring up into his expectant eyes, she was afraid her will just wasn't strong enough to overcome both the desire she saw reflected back and some instinct she'd thought long dead.

She nodded slowly, and his hand touched the small of her bare back, pulling her into the heat of his body. A hiss of breath surged through her teeth at the feel of his skin against her own. She'd loved the bridesmaid dress Karyn had chosen for her. Black floor-length velvet, elegant, sophisticated and perfect for the early December wedding. Very Anne. The neckline slashed from shoulder to shoulder, revealing a hint of her collarbone. The long sleeves and unadorned style hugged the curves of her body.

But the back of the gown was what she'd fallen in love with. Cut from one shoulder to the other, the curve dipped just to the bottom indent of her spine. From the front the gown was classic, from the back it was decadent. A perfect description for the two sides of her life— her past and her present merged into one.

She'd never been so grateful to be showing some skin.

Each of Blake's fingers branded her as they spread against the small of her back. Hot tendrils snaked up her spine. The vision of him dipping a single finger beneath the edge of her dress thrust into her brain, and a spike of need shot through her body.

"Enjoying yourself?" His voice was low and rough as he leaned into her space so he could get closer to her ear.

A wicked desire to tease him rolled through her, a bubble of energy inside her chest just bursting to get out. Or maybe that was the inner wild child she'd left behind ten years ago.

She leaned up onto her toes, pulling the heels of her four-inch Jimmy Choos off the floor and whispered into his ear, "Not yet," before biting the edge of his lobe.

His body jerked in surprise. But the hands at her back flexed, pulling her tighter against him. "Well, we can't have that, can we?"

She'd shocked him—and herself—but she'd aroused him, too. A satisfied smile played at the corners of her lips.

His eyes, the tempting color of her favorite rich chocolate fudge—an indulgence she rarely allowed— smoldered down at her. She'd met a lot of men in her life, but none of them had ever looked at her with that expression—a mix of desire, desperation, control and promise. If he hadn't been holding her, her knees just might have given out.

Strange that. In all her past encounters, she'd been the one to wield the power. Men had come to her either because of who she was or for her stunning face. She had no idea if Blake knew her real name, or rather her full name. She wondered for a second if it mattered. Probably not.

She had a decision to make.

Sinner or saint? Which was she tonight?

"WHERE'D YOU GET that tattoo?"

Blake Mitchell turned his head to look at the beautiful bombshell stretched across the bed behind him. With a long, slender finger, Anne Sobel traced the lines of the crouching tiger etched into the skin of his right shoulder.

He often forgot it was even there…but that was probably for the best.

"Prison."

He had no idea why he'd told her the truth…or part of the truth anyway. The tiger actually covered up a few crude markings. His family didn't even know about the months he'd spent in jail for assault and battery. They'd assumed he was on another military assignment. Probably because that's what he'd told them.

He hadn't wanted them to know the truth—that he'd beaten the shit out of his sister's rapist after the man had been found not guilty. They all knew the asshole had done it. But he'd been a football star, a veritable god for Mississippi State, and the jurors had been swayed by his squeaky-clean image and abundance of press.

Blake had been patient, waiting until the asshole was separated from the people and media protecting him. That patience hadn't prevented Blake's arrest, but at least it had kept his sister and family from knowing what he'd done. By the time the guy had come to and ID'd Blake, the press had moved on to an even bigger story and no one in California had cared that some guy had been bloodied and bruised.

Blake had done what he'd had to in order to protect his sister, and even knowing what it had cost him—his career with Special Forces—he'd make the same decision tomorrow.

Anne chuckled, pulling his attention back to where it should be—on her. The sultry sound of her laughter rushed through his body. They'd had sex once…but he wanted her again. With an urgency he didn't understand. From the moment she'd walked down the aisle today he'd been unable to see anything but her.

"Liar. Tell me the truth."

He should probably be grateful that she thought it was a joke. And that they were both buzzed enough on champagne and sexual satisfaction that by morning this moment would be fuzzy and far away. Maybe he'd simply needed to tell someone the truth. No one in his family could know what he'd done, and what it had cost him. He refused to add to Karyn's pain that way.

Rolling over, Blake pulled Anne beneath him on the rumpled hotel comforter and stared down into her upturned face. Bright green eyes, smoky black makeup smudged at the corners, stared back. She should have looked like a raccoon. Instead the effect made her eyes wide and slanted...mysterious. For some reason he wanted to see her naked—not just without clothes but without makeup, without anything but what God had given her. He had no doubt she'd be gorgeous.

He'd seen her shoes, the expensive streaks in her golden-blond hair, the expertly applied cosmetics, and knew they were her own brand of protection. Maybe he recognized them so easily because he had plenty of his own armor in place.

Or maybe he saw them because at this moment he wanted desperately to break beyond them, to see her as she truly was. They hadn't known each other long enough for that, though.

"I need to leave. It'll be dawn before I get home as it is." Anne yanked against his hold on her wrist, obviously uncomfortable under his silent scrutiny.

"Don't leave." He pressed his hips into the cradle of her body, pinning her to the bed with his weight. Her nipples puckered in quick response even as anger flared in her eyes. He reached down with his mouth, placing a kiss to the soft velvet skin at her shoulder. "It's snowing. Dangerous. Karyn would never forgive me if you wrecked."

She moved beneath him, a combination of desire and protest. He could smell the scent of her arousal. An answering haze of need bloomed inside him.

"Stay," he breathed just before his lips touched down on her wide mouth. Her eyes still glittered, a combination of pique and desire, as she opened to the onslaught of his persuasion. They warred, not with words but with tongues, thrusting, fighting, convincing. Her body undulated beneath him, loosening his hold on her hands until they finally jerked free.

He expected her to pull away. Instead, her fingers brushed down the length of his right shoulder, lightly tracing the outline of his permanent souvenir.

Smiling, he leaned back so he could look at her. "I would have thought you'd have some ink of your own, actually." She'd certainly been wild enough.

"Nope. Against the rules."

Trailing kisses down the center of her body, he loved the way she arched into his mouth, sensual and greedy for more. Her breath caught in the back of her throat, a little hiccup of air.

"I never figured you for the straight and narrow. In fact, I could have sworn you delighted in breaking rules."

Her eyes snapped to his, her body stilling beneath him. Her skin was still flushed with the heat of his touch and yet she turned away from him the only way she could, twisting her head so he couldn't look into her eyes. She was spread out beneath him, sensual and beautiful, but no longer in the moment with him. He didn't like that, didn't like knowing that something he'd said had dulled the glow of her desire.

He hadn't expected vulnerability from her. From the sophisticated and regal woman he'd watched all evening. From the sensual and demanding woman he'd had in his bed half the night. From the hellion the headlines had screamed about.

His protective urges reared up and told him to fix this. Now. Tucking his finger beneath her chin, he turned her back to face him. "Does it matter? Because it doesn't to me."

She knew exactly what he was saying. Her eyes narrowed as she studied him, looking into his eyes, searching his face.

"No." The single word was low and throaty. "I suppose it doesn't. Karyn told you."

It wasn't a question but he answered anyway, nodding. "She asked me to watch over you tonight."

She shook her head, a rueful smile tugging the corners of her lips. "Of course she did."

She drew in a deep breath. Blake's eyes fixated on the rise and fall of her breasts beneath him. He wanted to lean down and pull that teasing nipple into his mouth but wasn't sure of his reception.

Anne finally let the air go on a sigh that seemed to relax her. Her eyes traveled slowly up the length of his body, her kiss-swollen lips pulling into a mischievous smile as she reached for him. It was his turn to sigh when she wrapped the warmth of her palm around his aching erection.

"So, about that tattoo. I could have been lying." She arched up, rubbing her silky thighs against him. "Maybe you should check. Just to be sure."

Loving that idea, and the chance for some payback, he grasped her waist and flipped her onto her stomach. Kneeling between her open thighs, he spread them wide, enjoying the telltale glint of the arousal that coated her sex. But he didn't start there. Instead, he touched the base of her neck, beginning an excruciating exploration for any hidden marks. She gasped as he sucked at her nape and then blew a cooling stream of breath across the wet patch of her skin.

He rolled her head this way and that, tantalizing her with his fingers and mouth. Down the length of each arm, across her shoulders. Lavishing each tiny vertebra of her spine with individual attention. Her body squirmed beneath him, inflaming his desire, which was already riding the slippery edge of control.

Her skin was soft and fragrant. A delicious mixture of knowledge and need pulsed beneath the thin layer against his lips as he kissed the dip of her waist and the flare of her hips. He could almost feel the growing urgency heating her body beneath him.

Finally, he allowed them both the exquisite pleasure of touching her sex. She groaned low in her throat and pushed hard against his hand when he slid a finger inside her hot and slippery core.

Uninhibited, she greedily took the pleasure he gave her, forcing him back and fighting for more. He couldn't control her or himself. He couldn't wait to possess her, to feel her body take him in and hold him tight.

Turning her back over to face him, he grabbed a condom and rolled it down his cock. He was inside her within seconds, the exquisite feel of her heat surrounding him. She reared up with him, digging her fingernails into his back, trying to bring them closer together. She bit the edge of his bottom lip, sucking it into her mouth before soothing the ache with her tongue.

Meeting him thrust for thrust, she ground her hips against him, wrapping her legs around his body and holding him tight. They stayed that way, both straining for the unbelievable edge that they wanted to launch themselves over, pumping, pulling, chasing each other closer.

With a guttural groan of satisfaction, Anne dropped her head against the scattered pillows, her blond hair ballooning into a soft, disheveled cloud around her beautiful face. The orgasm ripped through her body—he could feel it, see it, practically taste the sweetness of it on his tongue. He enjoyed watching her shudder with the sensations, enjoyed knowing he was the source of her pleasure.

When she'd finally stilled beneath him, he let his own pleasure break free, shaking with the force of his restraint. He let the aftershocks of her orgasm haul him with her, the muscles of her inner walls massaging his sex in the most delicious way he'd ever known.

He looked down at the satisfied smile on her bliss-filled face and knew he was in trouble.

He didn't want to roll away, didn't want to lose the connection he'd found when they were locked together. He'd never had such an intense reaction to a woman in his life. Granted he was a little rusty. For the past several years he'd been preoccupied with building his business and hadn't had the time or inclination to play the dating game. One-night stands had been the name of his game.

But this was different. The woman beneath him had been the first thing to make his blood quicken since he'd stopped jumping out of perfectly functioning airplanes. She stirred, her eyes fluttering open. His entire body felt the impact as her brilliant green gaze caught his.

Oh yeah, he was in trouble.

2

AWARENESS CAME SLOWLY, crawling up Anne's spine along with a pounding headache and a sickening gurgle at the bottom of her stomach. The headache was all alcohol, although she hadn't really drunk that much.

The churning stomach, not so much.

She didn't even have to open her eyes, she could smell it. The maddening scent of professional-grade cleaner that could never quite be covered by the sickening floral spray they used to try and hide it. She'd once suggested to her mother that the hotel find another way to eliminate the smell. The woman had dismissed her suggestions. Surprise, surprise.

She hadn't noticed it last night, although she hadn't noticed much of anything besides the way Blake made her body burn.

Well, apparently it was time to pay the piper's price.

Her legs scraped against sheets that weren't her own yet were all too damn familiar. She opened her eyes. Keeping them shut wouldn't change things no matter how much she wanted it to. She took a halting tour of the space, trying to move only her eyeballs in deference to her protesting head.

Different, and yet still the same. The bedspread and artwork changed, but the impersonal still permeated every inch of the cookie-cutter hotel room.

Horrific memories slithered out from beneath the rock she'd shoved them under, making her stomach roil even faster. Maybe, if she could stay out of the bathroom, she could keep the worst of the images at bay.

The vision of her brother, dangling lifeless from the bathroom ceiling of their hotel suite, slammed into her brain anyway. Her muscles went rigid. Her lungs protested their sudden lack of oxygen as she forgot to breathe, forgot her surroundings, forgot everything but the nightmare. Curling her body into a ball, Anne shoved the heels of her hands into her eyes and laid her pounding head on her knees.

This was why she should have left last night. This was why she never stayed in a hotel. Not just Prescott hotels. Any hotel ever. After her brother's suicide, she'd run away from the chaos, the guilt, the madness of the life she'd once led. She'd changed her name from Annemarie Prescott to plain Anne Sobel.

It had taken her years but she'd finally built herself a new life with no help from her mother or her trust fund. A life she could be proud of. A life with meaning outside whether or not she had the latest "it" accessory.

The downside was that for years she'd lived in fear of someone discovering who she really was and turning the information over for a quick buck. It had been a long time before the paparazzi had given up trying to uncover her hidey-hole. Birmingham, Alabama—not exactly first on their list of places to look. But now the world had moved on and found a new party girl to glorify, giving Anne a little room to breathe.

Taking on another persona, adopting her mother's maiden name and pretending that Annemarie had never existed was worth it for a sense of peace.

And if she was lonely from time to time…well, that was a price she'd willingly pay again and again to be out from under her mother's thumb and away from the memories and the girl she'd once been. Even though she'd been surrounded by people, she'd been just as alone in her old life, anyway. Or she would have been, without her brother.

Now, if she could just get out of *here*.

"Aspirin."

The deep voice startled her, although she hadn't for a second forgotten that she wasn't alone. Her mind might have been swamped by nasty images of her past, but in some corner she'd been aware of Blake's presence in the room with her.

His cupped hand appeared above her face, the long, tanned arm blocking her view of everything else. This was possibly a good thing.

A water bottle slid into her line of sight, strong fingers wrapped around opaque sides. She reluctantly uncoiled her body, careful to keep the covers caught tight to her chest which seemed like a stupid thing to do, all things considered.

She took the little white pills, downed them with one cold swallow and finally looked at him. Blake Mitchell. Her best friend's older brother. The man she'd screwed six ways to Sunday last night.

Oh, she could blame it on the alcohol but she'd known, one-hundred-and-ten percent known, exactly what she was doing last night. And she'd wanted this man with a passion she hadn't felt in…years. Of course, that didn't exactly make what she'd done right.

Anne would be the first to admit that her upbringing had given her a skewed idea of what was appropriate. But even she knew that using her best friend's brother for meaningless sex crossed the line. Especially given her history. Karyn might not care…but that didn't take away the guilt gnawing at Anne's insides.

Inappropriate sex had always been her slippery slope.

She wondered if it was seeing Karyn and Chris together that had pushed her over the edge, or just being in Mother's hotel again. Either way, she'd obviously reverted to some very, very bad habits. Sexual pleasure could be just as much of a drug as crack cocaine.

Oh, she had sex. But in a very controlled environment with single men who understood that they were both simply getting off. No one got hurt. No one staked out her house to catch a compromising photo.

But with Blake, she hadn't been able to stop herself from taking what she'd wanted. And that was probably what scared her most. She'd been so careful to control her affairs before. This one had not been planned.

Even now, she couldn't keep her eyes away from him. His hair, burnt-toast brown, was disheveled. His chest was bare, hard and lean, and made her want to reach out and touch.

It would be so easy to lose herself in him again, to let him take the memories and the edge of bone-deep pain that being in this room caused her.

But she'd used Blake Mitchell enough last night. She couldn't do it again.

He sat on the bed beside her, his hip rubbing against

her own beneath the Egyptian-cotton sheets. She fought past the urge to reach out for him.

"Good morning." His voice was gruff, rusty. "Karyn and Chris are leaving in about fifteen minutes. Do you want to head down to see them off?"

With a silent nod, the only response she could manage between the desire, self-loathing and guilt swimming around inside her, she watched as he unfolded from the bed and disappeared into the bathroom.

Water sounded, the floor creaked against the weight of a full-grown male and the nightmares returned full force.

She couldn't stay. She needed out of here. *Now.*

Anne swung her legs over the side of the bed, stood up just a little too fast for her head's comfort and scanned the room. She was so worked up over Blake and the memories that it took several minutes to notice the bag in the corner. Her bag. The one that had been sitting in her trunk since she'd packed everything from Karyn's parents' place yesterday morning.

Ripping into it, she pulled out the first things she could find, a pair of well-worn jeans and a peach sweater. Clean panties and a bra helped make her feel somewhat human again. She brushed her hair, applied a minimum of makeup and finger brushed her teeth all in five minutes at the dresser mirror. She wasn't waiting. And the hounds of hell would have had to drag her into that bathroom.

She grabbed her dress out of the closet—she'd spent a lot of money on it and would be damned before she left it. Besides, she really did love it. She threw a glance at the closed bathroom door, considered yelling her good-bye at Blake but thought better of it. Not very romantic.

Besides, this way was better—he wouldn't feel obligated to pretend he wanted something more than one night.

Ten minutes after waking up, Anne walked out the door and right into the lobby full of Karyn and Blake's family.

Anne groaned. Any thought of skirting around the edges before anyone noticed her burned up in a flash as Karyn yelled across the large, echoing space.

"Anne. What are you doing here?"

"Ah." Her brain was working at a distinct disadvantage, but as her friend rushed forward it seemed to kick in.

"Snowstorm, remember. There was no way I could drive home in that."

Karyn slipped her arms around her in a big hug and squeezed tight, whispering in her ear, "Are you okay? You look a little pale."

Her friend leaned back, looked deep into her eyes and stared hard. Pinpricks of emotion she really didn't want to deal with stung the backs of her eyes. Only Karyn.

From the moment they'd met, both working at Walker Technologies, she'd recognized something deep inside Karyn—a twin to the suppressed pain and loneliness that resonated in her own chest. Karyn had been hiding the secret of her rape; Anne had been hiding the secret of who she really was. She disguised her pain with bright smiles and a bubbly personality. Karyn had camouflaged hers with silence and solitude. At least until she'd met Chris. He'd helped heal her wounds.

Anne was happy Karyn had found someone who could do that for her. She knew she'd live with her own scars for the rest of her life. That was okay. Nothing and no one could wipe away the guilt she carried.

"I'm fine. Really."

"I suppose you never have to worry about room availability when your mother owns the hotel."

Or when you shared. "Um, absolutely."

"Chris and I were about to leave. We're just waiting on Blake to come down." Karyn wrapped an arm around her shoulders and pulled her into the small knot of people standing around a conversation area.

Anne tried to fight the urge to run. Leaning into Karyn she said, "I need to head out now because I'm not sure how long it'll take me to get home in this snow and ice. You have a wonderful trip."

She kissed Karyn on the cheek, slung her bag over her shoulder and headed for the heavy etched-glass front door. Her mother had taste if nothing else. She was halfway there when the back of her neck began to tingle.

As she reached the door, Anne couldn't stop herself from turning around to look at him. His deep chocolate eyes were trained solely on her. The sensation was unnerving…and somehow left her feeling like a schoolgirl with her hand caught in the cookie jar.

His only reaction was a single raised eyebrow as the left edge of his luxuriant lips dipped down into a frown.

She jerked back around to face the door. Taking a steadying breath, she pushed against the cold glass and headed out into the freezing, lonely winter morning. The wind whipped by and stole her breath.

It was just her and her headache as she headed away from her mother's hotel, the memories it stirred and the first man to tempt her senses in a very long time.

Running away. Again.

Karyn was the only person in her new life who knew who she really was…well, and Blake now apparently.

But even then, knowing who she was didn't mean he understood.

Despite the emotional trauma that had immediately bonded them, even Karyn couldn't completely comprehend what her life had been like and always would be. Anne had learned early and quick to keep pieces of herself locked away—from her mother, from the media, from the moneygrubbing parasites that looked at her life of privilege and wondered what they could take from her. She'd used those lessons to keep her true identity safe. To close herself off from the life she wanted nothing more to do with.

She'd never have a normal life. A husband who loved her. A family of proud parents and overprotective brothers. She wasn't sure she could ever learn to trust someone enough to form the kind of bond that required. Hell, one night in a hotel room with a man had her turning tail to run.

She shrugged. It was her coping mechanism, the way she kept her mind and soul safe. It was something she'd come to grips with years ago, the limitations of her life. It had never bothered her before today.

So why did she now want more? It probably had everything to do with Karyn, her whirlwind romance and fairy-tale wedding. It couldn't have anything to do with Blake Mitchell.

And even if it did…it wouldn't matter. She'd never see the man again.

PETER BURG WATCHED as Annemarie Prescott slipped out the large double doors, a duffel bag slung over her shoulder. It had been easy to blend into the crowd last night, to observe as she mixed and mingled with the other wedding guests.

It had been a stroke of luck when word had come into the corporate offices that she'd pulled strings to reserve the ballroom for her friend.

A smile curved the edges of his lips. He knew for a fact that she hadn't reserved a room of her own in the hotel. He had the pictures to prove that she'd shared.

He wasn't exactly certain how they might come in handy but he figured it was good to be prepared. The more dirt he had on Annemarie, the more leverage he had over her; however he was going to keep the pictures of that man pressing her back into the wall of the hallway, his hands and mouth tugging at her dress, to himself for the moment.

The pictures themselves made his blood boil a little. Yes, she'd always been free with her body, which had bothered him. He'd long thought that she degraded herself for no good reason and resented the fact that the men she chose to do it with were trash.

Especially when he'd been standing before her, ready to worship at her feet.

Not anymore. She'd be the one groveling now, begging for his help when her world collapsed around her once more. And he'd do it, for a price.

He had plans for Annemarie Prescott. And he had no doubt that eventually she'd fall in line. He could be very persuasive…and patient.

Cold wind whipped inside his open coat as he quickly crossed to his car parked on the opposite side of the lot. He'd follow her home. He wanted to make sure she arrived there safely.

He needed her. At least for a little while.

3

BLAKE STARED out his windshield at the vacant town house across the street. He knew it was vacant, because he'd asked his sister where Anne would be today.

Karyn had been surprised to see him, to say the least. He lived in the next state over, so dropping by her house wasn't an everyday occurrence. And while they talked fairly regularly, he didn't make a habit of telling her—or any of his family—about his daily movements. At least not anymore. The family had been very close before Karyn had been raped.

While that incident had pulled them together to support her, it had also caused tension among them. Whenever he'd seen his mother, she'd talk only about how Karyn was doing. How her case was progressing. And those discussions had always increased the guilt and rage that crawled inside him.

Something he really didn't need. He'd pulled away from them—a form of punishment for his part in it all and protection for his sanity.

Shaking off the unwanted thoughts, he refocused on the modest brick building Anne called home. It surprised him. He'd expected her to live in a rambling mansion or an exclusive subdivision with a gate and guard shack, at least. The house was nice. Small, but she lived alone so it made sense. It wasn't wasteful or extravagant but it was in a good neighborhood.

He could easily get inside. But that wasn't why he'd come. He still wasn't sure that coming here had been the smart thing to do, but here he was.

It had been a little over a month since he'd last seen Anne, since she'd slipped through his fingers out that hotel door. Part of him had wanted to chase after her, to ask her why she'd thought it was necessary to leave like a thief while he was in the shower.

But he hadn't.

It had been a very long time since he'd had to chase after a woman. He wasn't in the habit of pursuing females who didn't want his attention—especially after what had happened to his sister—and it was clear that Anne wanted nothing more to do with him.

If he'd thought of her—often in the middle of lonely nights—that was his own problem.

Or it had been until Marie Prescott had called Mitchell Security.

After being court-marshaled four years ago for his assault-and-battery stunt, he'd been dishonorably discharged from the army and had to find another way to make a living. He'd been trained in surveillance, so opening a security firm had been a no-brainer. Things had been difficult to begin with—his history made hiring him for security a tough sell. But his superior officers and fellow soldiers had helped, sending him referrals whenever they could. Their support and understanding had meant so much.

Eventually his reputation and work had spoken for themselves. That and the fact that his case had been overturned on appeal—after he'd already left the army—and his discharge changed to honorable. But he'd never been so happy that the lean days were over as when he'd gotten the call from Anne's mother. He hadn't liked the way she's spoken to him. She was demanding. Entitled. Egotistical. She'd offered him money—lots of it—if he'd help bring her daughter home, and he'd delighted in declining.

So why was he sitting outside Anne's house?

Marie Prescott's warnings had niggled in the back of his brain until he couldn't concentrate for worry that the woman might be right. Marie had told him Anne refused to believe the threat was real and was ignoring her edicts to return home where she would be safe on the family compound.

That he could believe. Admittedly, he didn't know Anne all that well, but what he'd gleaned from their one night together was that she had an independent streak a mile wide and was unafraid and adventurous. Not the sort of person to be easily cowed.

However, the more he'd thought about it the more he'd worried. If Marie was telling the truth and something bad happened to Anne he wouldn't be able to live with himself.

He hadn't agreed to help Marie just yet. Why had she called *him?* Her answer when he'd asked had been that she thought his personal ties through Karyn might help in persuading her. That perhaps Anne would listen to someone she trusted more than she'd apparently listened to her mother. Little did the woman know he was likely the last person Anne wanted to see…or trust. But he couldn't simply ignore the situation if she really was in danger.

So he'd take a look around for anything suspicious.

He'd ask her if she'd noticed anything unusual. He wasn't exactly looking forward to the interview but life wasn't always pleasant. And, in truth, he really wanted to see Anne again. Maybe it would help him get her out of his head.

He glanced down at the clock on the dashboard—two o'clock. He had at least three or four hours before she'd be home from work, and he had no desire to corner her there. She'd made it clear she didn't want to see him, and his reason for being here wasn't likely to change her opinion. His showing up at her office would only add to the unpleasantness, not to mention her resistance. No sense in putting himself at a disadvantage before the conversation even began.

So it looked as if he had some time to kill.

Maybe he should go back and visit more with Karyn. Maybe she'd have some suggestions on how he could soften Anne up…. Ideas that wouldn't involve the use of his tongue and hands—as much as that disappointed— because something told him that he'd had his shot at her warming his bed. Unfortunately, it was all his deprived mind could come up with at the moment. Seducing her into submission.

ANNE PULLED into her parking spot, turned the key in the ignition and leaned her head back against the headrest. Home. Finally. A headache throbbed at the center of her skull, the result of skipping lunch and a meeting from hell.

She'd been excited to receive a promotion to VP of marketing right after the wedding. It had been a confirmation of her talent and a direct result of the hard work she'd put in at Walker Technologies over the past several years. She'd come to college late—starting at twenty—and had gone to work for Walker when she'd graduated four years later. Six years more and she was working her way up the corporate ladder.

Product placement, ad campaigns, market research, sales projections and tracking. She loved every minute of her job—although developing media campaigns had to be her favorite. It gave her a chance to use her media history for something other than bad memories.

The ironic thing was that it was precisely the kind of position she could have held at Prescott Hotels if her mother had ever thought she had the intelligence. Funny how she'd had to leave to find her success. Lucky for her that she'd also found contentment. Too bad for her mother, who still couldn't admit she'd been wrong about her daughter.

Thinking about her mother made the pounding in Anne's head increase to brain numbing. Marie had been the only parent—and Anne used the term loosely—in her life since her father had died in a car accident when she was four. She barely remembered him now—nothing but a fuzzy idea of what might have been.

She'd kept in contact with her mother over the past ten years, although that contact had been infrequent and as brief as possible. But suddenly that wasn't good enough—Marie had called her every day this week. What was making her mother so desperate?

Marie had been trying to get her back to the family estate for months, but something had obviously happened to increase the intensity of her machinations. The week had started with another edict, something Anne found easy to ignore. But then the cajoling had started. That was different. The concern over Anne's safety, a revelation that Anne was in danger from a stalker—

something Anne had seen no proof of—and finally the claim that Marie was ill.

She wondered what lie her mother would come up with next. And as much as she didn't want to, she wondered what the truth was.

Not that it mattered. When would Marie realize that nothing she offered or threatened could bring Anne home to New York? Birmingham was now her home. She had a job she enjoyed and was usually good at—apart from screwing up a report last week and prompting the meeting from hell this afternoon. She still had no idea how it had happened….

She was independent and happy. And she was going to stay that way. One trip home and her freedom would end. She knew it to the soles of her feet. She'd needed every bit of strength and determination she had to escape the world of excess and privilege. If her mother got her hooks into Anne again she'd never let go. The only reason she'd gotten away the first time was because her mother had counted on Anne's inability to live without money and things and people at her beck and call.

Marie had been wrong, something that made Anne smile every time she thought of it. It wasn't often her mother was wrong and she delighted in being one of the only people who'd never fallen into line.

Really, running away ten years ago had been Anne's final step in a lifelong quest to thwart her mother's fight for control.

Those first few months when the transition had been difficult, she'd used that thought to get her through. Her mother wouldn't win. She wouldn't let her. Not after what the woman had pushed Anne's brother, Michael, to do.

If Marie had shown one ounce of warmth or maternal

concern when Michael had gone to her, Anne knew in her heart her brother never would have hung himself.

Pushing back the unwanted memories, she walked inside her house, flipping switches as she went. There was something about light in the first gloom of dusk that always made her feel warm and safe. The tension that had tightened her shoulders began to ease. But the place was freezing. Shivering, she wrapped her arms around her middle and huddled further into her coat. She didn't remember turning down the heat before she'd left this morning. Maybe the unit had finally given up. She'd been fighting with it for over a year but had hoped to baby it along until her tax refund came in sometime next month.

Depositing her purse and briefcase on the hall table, she headed through the open-plan living room toward the thermostat and stopped dead in her tracks.

The back door at the end of the long hallway stood wide open. The doorjamb surrounding the lock plate was shredded. The door wasn't much better, a half-moon of splinters was all that was left of the knob.

Oh hell. Panic rushed into her, squeezing her lungs and making her heart beat against the suddenly too small walls of her chest. She reached down and grabbed the first thing her hand settled on, the back of a well-loved recliner. She gasped for air, but couldn't seem to get enough of it.

Stop it, she told herself. *Hyperventilating won't get you anywhere.* Glancing quickly around her, she took stock. A couple of the bottom doors on her built-in were hanging wide open, books and papers falling out in a messy pile to the floor. Shards of glass glittered against the carpet. Who knew which knickknack they'd once been. But her expensive TV still sat on the stand on the far side of the room. Too heavy to carry out?

Something long, slender and glinting silver lay in the hall at the archway to her kitchen. Big, sharp, dangerous knife or the handle to her frying pan? She wasn't going to stick around to find out.

Anne backed slowly toward the front door, snatching her purse and cell phone off the hall table as she went. Outside to call the police. And Karyn. And possibly stay with her…and her brand-new husband of four weeks when they'd just returned from their extended honeymoon a week ago. Yeah, probably not. She'd figure something out.

Reaching behind her, Anne felt for the doorknob, letting out a silent sigh of relief when her searching fingers finally touched it. But a single sound stopped her.

Mrreow.

"Shit!" Slapping a hand over her mouth to hold in any other sounds, she stood with her back pressed tight against the door and waited…for what she wasn't sure. For some masked man to come barreling into the room and throw her to the ground? For ninjas to erupt through the back windows? For her cat to silently pad from the kitchen to wind her skinny, wrinkled body around her ankles.

"Prada." The name pushed out of her lungs as she leaned down, grabbed her cat and buried her face in the hairless skin.

Okay. If Prada was fine she could deal with the rest of it. After finally exiting the house, Anne raced to the safety of her car, slammed all the locks shut, placed Prada on the seat beside her and called the police.

Pressing the phone to her ear, Anne tried to calm her

breathing so she could hear through the harsh in and out. "Nine-one-one. What's your emergency?"

"I'd like to—" Her words were cut off midstream by a scream so loud it echoed off the windows and bounced through the car. The response was involuntary, a knee-jerk reaction to someone tapping loudly on the window next to her head.

"Ma'am? Are you all right? Ma'am? What's wrong?" The voice on the other end of the line sharpened with concern.

"I'm sorry." Anne's eyes narrowed as she looked through the driver's side window of her Miata to find Blake Mitchell staring back at her. What the hell was he doing here? Now? At the exact moment she needed him?

No, that wasn't right. She didn't need him. She didn't need anyone. She was fine.

Glaring at him, she turned away and continued talking to the dispatcher. "Someone just scared me. I need to report a break-in at my town house."

"Are you in any danger? Are you inside the home? Is the intruder still there?"

"No, I'm fine. I'm outside in my car. I'm not sure if anyone is still inside. I didn't stick around to find out."

The dispatcher took her address and said an officer would be there shortly. After assuring the woman that she didn't need to stay on the phone with her until their arrival, Anne shut off her phone and sat staring through her windshield for a moment. Her pulse was finally dropping, which was good because she wasn't sure her heart could handle any more ups and downs in one day.

Taking a deep breath, she turned her head to find

Blake right where she'd left him, leaning against the side of her car, one arm propped on the roof, positioned slightly behind the window so he'd been out of her line of sight. She wasn't entirely certain that had been an accident.

His dark-chocolate eyes stared down at her, watchful, assessing. She wasn't sure she liked that at all. It gave her the sensation of being weighed and measured, as if he could see everything inside her even if she didn't want him to.

Definitely not pleasant. She much preferred when his eyes smoldered.

She dug in her purse for keys, then popped them into the ignition and cranked the car for power before rolling down her window. For some reason, she wanted to keep the closed door firmly between them. His eyes narrowed and one eyebrow lifted. She had the distinct impression he found her caution amusing.

Cold January air gushed through the opening. Another reason to keep her butt firmly in the car. She turned the heat up.

"What are you doing here?"

"I came to see you. And I'm guessing by the way you bolted out of that house like your ass was on fire that you're in a bit of a jam."

A bit of a jam. Ha! "Why?"

"Why are you in a bit of a jam? I don't know. You tell me."

"Why did you come see me? Now." Four weeks, three days and nine hours after he'd let her walk away.

"I was in Huntsville for a consultation, thought I'd stop by and see Karyn since I was so close."

"She's not here."

"Apparently. I talked to her earlier."

So if he wasn't here to track down his sister… "How did you know where I live?" Her brain, sluggish from the scare, finally caught up. Waving her hands, she cut off his response, answering her own question, "Never mind. Karyn told you."

A deep sound rolled from the center of his chest. It reminded her of the sound Prada made when she deigned to allow Anne to pet her. It wasn't an outright laugh… more of a quiet admission of amusement. "No, actually, she didn't. I own a security firm. Finding people is part of my job."

"So…what, you looked me up on the internet?"

His only response was a shrug.

Damn it. She could only guess at the shit he'd found. Because surely he hadn't resisted the urge to look up the exploits of her alcohol-and-drug-soaked sexcapades. After all, everyone else wanted to know.

"Entertained?" Her lip curled up in disdain, for both him and herself. Anger and embarrassment twisted inside making her a bit harsh. "So you decided to pop by for an unannounced visit a month after we screwed each other's brains out, why?" And why now? It wasn't exactly the most convenient time for her to receive visitors.

"Well, that's a flattering visual."

"You prefer sex? Just sex?"

"I don't think you can call it just sex when the marathon session goes for five hours and leaves my brain fuzzy the next morning."

What the hell was she doing? She was fighting—and flirting if she was honest—with a man she barely knew, sitting in her car outside her very broken into town house, while she waited for the cops.

"Forget it. I don't care why you stopped by. Now isn't a great time. Go away."

"No."

"What do you mean no?" Had she exited her house into an alternate universe? Or maybe she was still asleep. That was it. It would certainly explain the crappy sales report she'd gotten raked over the coals for—she never made mistakes like that. A nightmare tied to hearing her mother's voice every day for a week. If she lost her job, her mother would only insist harder that she come home.

And the ransacked house. Another dig at her security.

And the sexy-as-hell devil with the deep chocolate, bite-me eyes and stubborn demeanor who had shown up on her doorstep after a month? That was just too many lonely nights of lustful thinking.

This was all a nightmare…or maybe this last part was more a dream. She'd wake up any minute, Prada would beg her for breakfast and she'd race off for her morning Starbucks.

"Not until you tell me what's going on."

Or maybe not. Sighing, she said, "Someone broke into my place. I'm waiting here for the police to show up. Thanks to you scaring me half to death and making me scream in the dispatcher's ear, I would guess they'll be here shortly."

Blake reached inside her open window, ran his hand a little too close to the side of her breast for sanity, and unlocked the car doors.

It was a sad state of affairs. Her brain shortcircuited at the nearness of his hand, leaving her stupid and powerless as he walked around to the passenger side, opened the door and plopped his butt into her front seat. She'd clearly had enough time to lock his ass out in the cold. If she'd thought of it.

Instead, a laugh—probably hysteria—bubbled up inside her chest at the look of absolute horror he gave the spitting, clawing sack of skin in his hands. He held the cat as far in front of him as the console would allow. "Why do you have a skinned squirrel in your car?"

Reaching over, she snatched her baby from his hands. "Prada is not a squirrel." She turned her focus to the cat and held her up to coo at her, "Are you, baby?" She did it more because she knew it would bother him than for anything else. How she knew this, she had no idea, but she was dead certain it would.

And the curl of his lip and squint in his eyes proved her right.

"She's a hairless cat." Placing the cat in her lap, the black-pink-and-white mottled ball of skin curled up, keeping her eyes firmly on the man who'd dared to pluck her up from her comfy seat.

He watched, a mixture of horror and bewilderment on his face. "Why do you have a hairless cat?"

She shrugged, continuing to run her hand down the rough skin in rhythmic strokes. "Her original owners bought her because it was trendy, but then decided she was too much trouble to keep, so they took her to the shelter. But no one wanted her. The shelter volunteers said everyone thought she was ugly." It had broken her heart to see the tiny, shivering thing stuck in a corner cage, away from everyone else. She'd watched as several children had ignored Prada, opting for the cute and cuddly kittens with their wide take-me-home eyes. It had stirred something inside her. Prada deserved a chance to have a warm and loving family.

"That thing *is* ugly."

She looked over at him in disgust. No one ever looked beyond Prada's unusual exterior to the fiercely loyal soul beneath. Just another reason they never would have worked. Want her body? Love her cat.

"She's not ugly…. She has personality." Prada sighed, a discordant sound that cut through the car, and closed her eyes for a nap. Anne wouldn't admit it out loud, but the cat was sort of a spoiled brat.

The silence stretched out around them. It wasn't a comfortable silence, the kind that left you lax and somehow in tune with the person next to you. There was too much friction, too much male sexuality emanating off him for her to be comfortable.

What she wanted was for him to go away. No, that wasn't true. What she wanted was to take him upstairs— to hell with the ninjas—and let him give her libido another mind-blowing workout. What she *needed* was for him to go away. Because she couldn't deal with this— with him, too—right now.

She wanted him with a fierceness that had apparently sharpened in the month since she'd seen him, not lessened. The problem was that she shouldn't. They weren't good for each other. He made her feel things she'd left in her past. He made her want to abandon everything and lock them both into a room with a bed for the next month…or twelve.

She couldn't think of anything but him when he was so close.

So he needed to go. Turning her head, she looked at the man sitting beside her. Comfortable. Cocky. Solid as a damn bull.

"What do you want, Blake? You didn't come here looking for Karyn. It's way too late to contact me about our night together. Why are you here?"

He opened his mouth to answer her. She could see it would be something pat. It was written in his eyes. You could never lie to a champion liar.

"No bullshit."

He snapped his mouth closed again and stared at her for several seconds. She realized the minute he decided to tell her the truth, because his face took on a pinched look and his eyes went all soft and apologetic.

The expression shouldn't have looked good on him. Blake Mitchell was made to be a hard man. He had the body—tall, broad and thick with muscle. He had the attitude—confident, as if he was ten feet tall and bulletproof. But that touch of softness, of regret, made him more human somehow.

It also tied her stomach in knots. She wasn't going to like whatever he was going to say.

"Your mother asked me to bring you home."

4

BLAKE WATCHED as her entire body went rigid. Her jaw. Her hands. Even the muscles in her thighs. Not that he should be looking. Not now anyway. It was like lighting the fuse on a bomb and then getting distracted by the beauty of a sunset.

Stupid and pointless.

"Funny. I don't remember Mother having an office in Huntsville."

"What?" Shaking his head, he realized he needed to focus. He had no idea what she was talking about and that was a quick way to disaster. He was probably already headed there but...

"You said you met with a client in Huntsville before coming here. I didn't realize Prescott Hotels had an office in Huntsville."

The lightbulb flipped on. Damn she was quick.

"They don't."

The sirens of a police cruiser wailed in the distance, saving him from having to come up with more of a response. Those sirens were the perfect reminder that Blake could no longer question her mother's words. Anne was in serious trouble.

And he was going to help her whether she wanted him to or not. He would not let someone hurt her. He still wasn't certain that meant taking her home to her mother, but one issue at a time.

The first one being her look of skepticism. "I didn't lie. I met with another client. A government contractor worried about securing classified documents."

"Uh-huh." The sounds became louder as the police car pulled into the parking lot for Anne's complex. "Go away, Blake. I don't need or want you here. I don't care what my mother wants, either. I'm not going home."

Hopping out of the car—that drowned rat cradled to her chest—she slammed the door in his face. Frowning, he followed slowly behind Anne to where she and a cop stood close together.

The man was middle-aged with his blue Birmingham Police Department uniform shirt stretched over a slightly bulging belly. He was listening intently as Anne shared the details of the break-in.

Taking a step closer, Blake positioned Anne in the shelter of his body, almost touching her shoulder with his chest. He used his height to protect and claim. He couldn't say why, but the urge had been there and no desire to fight it had surfaced.

The maneuver earned him a glare from Anne, something that actually made his mouth twitch into a grin. What was it about needling her that made him smile?

He kept his mouth shut though. He had nothing of importance to add to the conversation and he'd learned a long time ago that listening always netted more information than talking.

"Let me take a look around first, then if everything is clear we can go inside and speak some more."

Anne nodded and they both watched as the officer

strode toward her house. The tension was back in her muscles. Hell, he could have cut wood across her shoulders they were so tight.

Without thought, he reached for her, offering the comfort and support of his arms. This was harder for her than she was letting on. He could only imagine the turmoil and sense of violation she must be fighting, something that had likely been a daily part of her life when she'd been Annemarie Prescott. But she'd put that behind her until today.

To his surprise, she let him tug her close. His arms wrapped around her stomach, her back nestled snuggly to his chest.

"I'm sorry, Annie."

A shiver tore through her. His reaction was immediate and intense, his cock jerking stiff at the smallest rub of her body against his own. He fought back a groan and hoped she was too preoccupied to notice.

Her chest expanded on a deep inhalation of breath. She held it for a second before finally letting it all go in a slow, smooth stream of air. Then she stepped free of his arms and turned to face him.

Her expression was blank. Her eyes, deep, dark green, were dull in a way that concerned him.

"I'm fine, Blake. I'll be fine. You can go."

He wondered who she was trying to convince, him or herself.

"I'm not going anywhere. You shouldn't have to face this alone."

"I've dealt with a hell of a lot worse alone. One amazing night in the sack does not give you the right to barge into my life. I've managed just fine without you for ten years, without anyone. I can manage this, too."

He had no doubt that she could. Beneath the blond-bombshell exterior, the designer pumps and the tailored clothes was a spine of steel. He admired that about her, her own inner strength.

The officer came back. "Whoever broke in is long gone. Why don't we go inside out of the cold, ma'am, so I can ask you a few more questions?"

It didn't slip his notice that the other man hadn't included him in the suggestion.

He followed anyway saying, "Amazing, huh?" to her back. "Yeah, that's a good description for that night. I probably would have used spectacular, though."

WHY WOULDN'T HE go away? Didn't she have enough to deal with?

Anne wasn't happy about his reasons for coming to see her. Okay, she'd admit that her ego had taken a bit of a hit over that one. He hadn't come because he'd been unable to get their night together out of his mind. Instead he'd come because her mother had probably paid him an obscene amount of money.

Why Blake? Why now?

Why couldn't her mother leave her the hell alone?

"It appears the intruder forced entry in through the back door."

No joke.

The officer seemed to be waiting for a reply. What could she say? *Brilliant deductive reasoning, Sherlock?* Glancing over at Blake, she realized he would be no help at all when he simply lifted an eyebrow at her.

Mumbling something appropriate, she waited for the officer to continue. The picture he made was almost comical—he was so out of place sitting on her dainty rose-velvet sofa. His butt was barely on the edge of the thing and he looked as if he was either ready to bolt—not what you want from the cop handling your case—or he was afraid the sofa would collapse beneath him. Again, not reassuring. She liked her furniture set. She'd found it at an estate auction and reupholstered the pieces herself. They were very feminine and frilly and far from the heavy lines and modern furniture her mother had always insisted on.

They were old, had a history. They'd belonged to a family who had laughed, cried and lived life on them. And now they were hers.

In contrast to the police officer, Blake was kicked back on one of the matching chairs, a boot-clad ankle crossed over his knee, intense eyes taking in every last detail before him. If anyone should worry about crushing the delicately carved wood and fabric, it was him. Was he worried? Nope. Ego or confidence? Did it really matter? The man looked right at home in her precious space. Damn it.

"Is anything missing, Ms. Sobel?"

Anne tore her attention away from Blake, berating herself for getting distracted by him…again.

"Not that I've noticed on this floor. There are several things out of place but nothing I can find missing. The electronics are still here."

"What about upstairs?"

"Well, I haven't been up there yet, but I can't think of anything impor—"

With a gasp and a feeling in her stomach as if someone had tied a rock to it and thrown it over a bridge, she raced upstairs. Tearing into her bedroom, she opened the closet doors and let out a sigh of relief when she pulled down the bins—full. Everything right where it was supposed to be.

Her designer collection: Jimmy Choo, Manolo, Prada, Hermès, Louis Vuitton, Kate Spade.

These were the only things she'd kept from her previous life. Slipping into those shoes, pulling out a new designer handbag…it always made her feel pretty and special. Each new purchase had cost her months of saving, but it was her one indulgence.

Sitting heavily on the bed, she balanced one box on her knee and sighed.

A sound at the door caught her attention and she snapped her head around to find Blake standing in the doorway to her bedroom.

She was an idiot. There was just no other way to explain why her body responded to the thought of him here, in her space. Her breasts began to tingle and an ache she'd been ignoring for weeks settled deep and hard at the center of her sex.

But apparently she was the only one experiencing the need for a quick repeat of their night together, because instead of undressing her with his eyes—which is what her body wanted him to do—he was shaking his head in disbelief.

"Shoes. Purses."

"Hey, buddy, don't knock the importance of designer leather goods. In fact…" An idea sparked as her eyes raced across the contents of the box on her lap. Snapping open the lid, she dug into one of the neatly arranged boxes and lifted out a pair of Prada pumps, nothing fancy from the front, but the heel was spindle thin and shaped like the stem of a flower. The petals, a throbbing hot pink, unfurled around the heel of the shoe. They were sexy and sophisticated. She always felt like a million bucks when she wore them.

If there was ever a time she needed an extra boost of confidence, it was now.

"What are you doing?"

"What does it look like? Changing my shoes."

"Now?"

She shrugged. He wouldn't understand.

Placing the box back on its shelf, she pushed past Blake and went downstairs.

"Nope, nothing is missing."

She wasn't a complete idiot. She had glanced inside her office on the way past to make sure that the computer, printer and fax were all still there. However, those could have easily been replaced. Some of the shoes in her collection she'd had since she was sixteen. They were irreplaceable works of art.

A scowl marred the officer's face as he followed her progress back to her seat.

"Can you think of any reason someone might want to scare you? Upset you? Hurt you?"

They spoke at the exact same time, Anne saying, "No," Blake blurting "Yes."

She glared across at him, telepathically telling him to shut his big mouth. "No."

He ignored her. "Do you know Anne's real name?"

The other man looked startled for several seconds before his face shuttered and he slowly answered, "Apparently not."

"Meet Annemarie Sobel Prescott, the heir to the Prescott Hotel fortune."

The officer's eyes went huge in his face and Anne just sighed. Another person who knew her identity. Another potential leak. Another person who might contact the gossip rags and reveal her location. Sure, it had been ten years, but she could just see the headlines now—Missing

Heiress Found in Podunk, Alabama. Some people might view her certainty at being front-page news as egotistical self-aggrandizing. She saw it as reality. The way she'd disappeared…hell, Mother hadn't even known where she was for months.

Besides, Prescotts were always newsworthy.

"Her mother recently asked me to bring her back to the family compound in New York. There have been threats against her life."

"Bullshit."

Both men turned to stare at her. She supposed the phrase hadn't been exactly ladylike. Too bad.

"My mother simply wants me, and you—" she looked pointedly at Blake "—to dance to her tune. She's been trying for months to get me home and that lie is just the last in a long line of them. Have you seen proof of these supposed threats against me?"

It was Blake's turn for pointed glances as he stared behind her, at the splintered edges of her back door.

"Coincidence. No one knows I'm here."

"I found you. Rather easily."

"You knew where to start looking. It wasn't exactly a needle-in-a-haystack hunt."

Apparently deciding to break up the heated discussion before it escalated, the officer cleared his throat and asked, "Has anything else happened recently?"

"No." She glared at Blake.

"Well, this report will be on file. I'm sorry to say that I don't expect much to come of it. Nothing was taken. Although, I will send a crime-scene tech out to collect evidence." He rose from the sofa, sticking his hand out. "Ms. Prescott."

"Ms. Sobel."

The smile on his face faltered for a moment before

he regained his composure. "Ms. Sobel. Please be sure to report anything else out of the ordinary that occurs, no matter how small it seems. If Mr...."

"Mitchell."

"If Mr. Mitchell is correct, then establishing a pattern of harassing behavior will be important."

"Thank you."

Anne walked the man to the front door and stood staring at it for several seconds after she'd closed it behind him.

She didn't want to turn around, walk back into that room and deal with Blake. Or rather, she didn't want to deal with the fight she knew was coming. Holding out against her mother was one thing. Would she be able to stand her ground against Blake, too? Especially when all her body wanted to do was melt into him?

He didn't give her much time to build her defenses. His voice sounded behind her, forcing her to face him.

"Go pack whatever you need. I'll call around and make a hotel reservation."

No, he wouldn't. "I am not staying in a hotel." Her voice was adamant and disdainful, more so than she'd meant it to be. It was a knee-jerk reaction, reverting to what she'd always thought of as the Prescott Tone of Voice. When she was growing up, it had gotten her whatever she'd wanted.

She immediately regretted using it. She'd learned that simple courtesy went much further than any regal facade she'd perfected. But when she was cornered...

"Oh? The local Motel 6 not good enough for little miss silver-spoon-in-her-mouth?"

His attitude wasn't helping any, either. "Let's just say that the last time I was in a hotel it did not end well."

Blake's face hardened. Her stomach tied in knots, her body catching on to the problem long before her brain did. "And whose fault was that?"

She was taken aback by his tone and the way he'd referred to her brother's suicide. "Is that supposed to be a comment about my brother?"

"Your brother? How would he have anything to do with our night together?"

With a groan, she realized they'd been talking about two completely different things. Understandable from his point of view. How to explain it to him, though, without bruising his ego? The only experience she immediately linked to a hotel was finding her brother's lifeless body. Of course, to him that would probably mean their night together had been completely forgettable. So far from the truth. But she wasn't sure he needed to know that.

"Sorry. I always associate hotels with finding my brother after he committed suicide. That's what I think about first, last, always. Honestly, it has nothing to do with you."

He took a step towards her, his outstretched hand offering her comfort she didn't want to take. He started in on the normal platitudes, "I'm so sorr—"

But she cut him off before he could finish, unwilling to accept the compassion she knew would be lurking in his eyes. She didn't deserve it. Instead she filled the silence with random words she really hadn't meant to say. "You were amazing. More than amazing. The best sex I've ever had. And trust me, I've had plenty of sex. Good sex. Bad sex. Forgettable sex. Nothing about you is forgettable." Her voice trailed to nothing before she finally snapped her mouth shut.

Better late than never.

"Well, I suppose that's something. Fine, no hotel. Karyn's place?"

"No. I am not barging in on your sister and her four-week-old marriage. The last thing she and Chris need right now is an unexpected guest."

"You know the minute you tell her what's happened she's going to insist you come to her place, especially because I'm guessing she already knows about your… phobia."

"Which is why I'm not telling her. This is my problem. I'm a big girl. I can handle this."

He frowned. "I never said you couldn't. But you don't have to do it alone. I'm here and we'll figure this out together."

It shouldn't matter that he was being nice and supportive. But it did. It meant a lot to her that there was someone here to…not lean on, but at least share the burden with.

And she was being nasty and snide. Sighing, she said, "I suppose you could help me secure the door. I'll call around in the morning and see if I can get a replacement. Until then…"

"Done. Shouldn't take much, I saw a pile of wood out back."

It took her a second to realize why that statement started warning bells clanging in her head. "When were you behind my building?"

"This afternoon." He grinned at her. Honest to God grinned, like a little boy who'd been caught covered in mud. He didn't even try to hide the inherent implications to his statement.

"You were here this afternoon? At my place? When I was at work?"

"Yep."

Anger welled up inside her. Oh, she'd been fighting it off and on since she'd walked in and seen her broken back door. The sense of security and normalcy she'd worked hard to build had been shattered in one afternoon. She had no idea where the thought came from, but she suddenly had to make certain he wasn't responsible for the loss.

"Did you do this?"

"Did I…do you mean did I break into your house? No! Why would I do something like that?"

"I don't know." And she honestly didn't. "Maybe so that you could get close to me again."

He moved across the room with long, smooth strides that suddenly had her feeling like prey. But she refused to give an inch to his obvious intimidation tactic. Still, when he stopped, his body looming over hers, she couldn't prevent her blood from quickening.

"We both know I could have come after you any time I wanted. You were the one who ran away, Anne. I just chose not to chase."

"Until now."

"I stopped chasing women a long time ago."

He leaned in closer, infiltrating her personal space with his body heat, his masculine confidence. She wanted to hate him for that alone. But her betraying body wouldn't let her.

"I don't have to."

Turning on his heel, he stalked out her back door, letting the mutilated wood quiver back and forth from the power of his exit. Within seconds he was back. She watched as he deftly secured her door, giving him one-word answers when he requested a hammer and nails. Five minutes. The man had barely spent any time at all doing something that would have surely taken her much longer.

"Thank you." Her words were hard and reluctant. He probably should have stretched it out if he'd wanted sincere appreciation. Her temper hadn't quite cooled off yet.

This time she was the one who turned away, heading for the front door as he cleaned up. She waited for him to approach, reaching for the handle so she could open the door and have him gone. She needed space so she could process what had happened.

So she could break down.

"I appreciate—"

His hand flattened on the door before it could open wider than an inch. Closing it, he blew up her night yet again.

"I'm not going anywhere, Anne. I'm staying right here."

5

"THE HELL YOU SAY."

Blake watched as her hand tightened over the knob, her knuckles turning red then white. She was angry. Not that she didn't have every right to be.

Pulling his gaze from her fingers, he tracked up her body until he was staring into her lush green eyes. Part of him felt sorry for doing this to her, for adding to her misery.

Not enough to leave her vulnerable though. "I am not leaving you here alone, Anne. You're stuck with me."

Frustration colored her cheeks as he turned his back. Better to just walk away and let her get used to the idea. She was a smart woman. In a few minutes she'd realize he was right and she was wrong. Not that she'd be happy with the situation.

In an effort to distract himself from the sexual frustration and mental torture he'd just sighed up for, Blake finally looked at his surroundings. Earlier, he'd been preoccupied with looking for signs of danger. Now, he could see the personal touches Anne had added to her home.

Her living room was formal, feminine but somehow

comfortable. The dainty furniture shouldn't have fit the woman she was, but the rich fabrics and lush colors helped to make the space inviting.

He knew firsthand how deceptive the appearance of her couch was. The thing was actually pretty comfy. He hadn't meant to but the moment he'd sat down he'd sort of sunk into it, deep velvet wrapping around him in a warm hug.

There were knickknacks, pretty things with zigzags and doo-dads and things that sparkled. He spotted several pictures scattered about, Karyn and Chris in several of them. There was a lone print on the far wall—Anne as a child. The little girl with bright blond ringlets was smiling but he could tell she really hadn't wanted to. Her hands wrapped around the shoulders of a small boy. She stood close, her body leaning into his, her fingers settled heavily on his shoulders. It almost looked as if she was protecting him.

The picture was the only visible touch of her previous life. She'd gone to great lengths to separate herself from the girl she'd once been.

And he suddenly realized just how difficult it was going to be to get her to agree to go home.

He no longer had any doubts about whether she was in danger. The question was, where would she be safest?

Clearly, her place had little to offer in the way of security. Sure, she had a run-of-the-mill security system. The kind that any half-wit with access to the Internet could figure out how to circumvent.

With just his presence, he could offer another layer of protection, but something told him she wouldn't appreciate him being the white to her rice.

It didn't take a genius to realize that the family compound in Upstate New York was probably protected like Fort Knox. Marie Prescott had a personal security team whose sole reason for existence was to prevent the riffraff from invading her space.

Anne would be safer there. But Blake realized the only way to get her there was kicking and screaming. He didn't quite understand the reasoning behind that but he didn't have to in order to know it was the truth.

Maybe if he did understand he could work around her....

In the meantime, he needed her to at least admit that everything was not right with her world. The first step and all.

Anne hadn't moved. For the few minutes he'd surveyed her space, the heat of her unhappy gaze had burned into his back. Okay, she wasn't simmering down. In fact, glancing over his shoulder at her, he expected to see fire burst through her skin. She was that upset.

What she needed was to blow her top...or alternately to break down and cry, but he couldn't see Anne doing that.

All right, he'd give her a target. Plopping his rear back down on her sofa, Blake crossed his arms behind his head, kicked back, and dangled his feet off the other end. Out of nowhere, the scrawny sack of bones she called a cat jumped on top of him and began kneading. Three seconds later it was curled up on his chest and, he would swear, snoring.

He looked over at her, his expression of disbelief morphing to a satisfied grin at the shock and awe on her face. He shimmied his shoulders, digging into the sofa for a nice long stay. He wasn't going anywhere.

With a sound somewhere between a screech and a groan, she walked toward him. It was a pity that she stopped just out of his reach or he'd really have pushed her over the edge by tumbling her into his lap, sack of bones or not. As it was, he just cocked his head to the side and watched her.

"You'll have to leave sometime. You don't even have any clothes."

"I have a bag in the car. Beside, didn't you know? I was Special Forces. I've been muddy, wet, cold and miserable. I can survive for days with nothing but dental floss, a yo-yo and a candy bar. This is the lap of luxury."

Okay, so he was exaggerating, but she didn't know that. He could understand why she wasn't thrilled with the situation. If he was honest, neither was he. The tension snapping between them was filled with mixed emotions that had the hairs on the back of his neck standing on end.

He didn't know what he wanted more, to drag her into his space and remind her what their night together had been like or to shake her until she gave him an honest answer as to why she'd run away from him. Or maybe he just wanted to hold her and tell her that it was all going to be okay.

He'd witnessed plenty of traumatic events, other people's traumatic events; he recognized the emotions bubbling up inside her. Beneath the layer of anger she was using right now to hold herself together were countless emotions—insecurity and fear at the forefront.

At some point the dam would break. Part of him really didn't want to be around for that. He didn't think he could take seeing that kind of vulnerability from his blond bombshell. She was strong. Independent. Fearless.

She took one more step forward, her eyes spitting

fire. "Don't make me call back the nice officer and kick your ass out."

"Don't make me call your mother."

Snatching up something on the table beside his head, she turned away from him and with a growl threw whatever it had been at the tiled entry floor. Small shards of glass bounced around, the tiny tinkle of sound somehow inappropriate and dissatisfying.

She stood silently staring down at the destruction. Her chest heaved on each labored breath and part of him worried she was finally crying.

He sat and watched, knowing that the last thing she'd want was for him to offer her anything, especially comfort. To his relief, when she finally turned back to face him, her cheeks weren't wet. Her face had paled from the livid red of her anger.

"I'm sorry." Her words were reluctant, almost as if she didn't really mean them but felt some obligation to say them.

He shrugged. "At least you didn't throw it at me."

"It was touch and go for a minute."

He laughed. Her honesty was one of the things he most admired about her. It was one of the things the paparazzi had loved about following her around. If they'd asked her a question, Anne had answered and answered truthfully, no matter the consequences. No matter who might care or who she'd offend.

He wondered what part of the trait had been her knowledge that the world moved differently for Prescotts. Or what part the desire to piss her mother off had played. But apparently, some part of it had simply been her innate distaste for bullshit.

That he could appreciate.

"Why don't you go upstairs, take a nice hot shower while I make us something to eat?"

It would relax her and allow her a few minutes alone. It would also give him time to call into the office and arrange for Marcus, his second in command, to manage things for the next few days. It had the added benefit of giving him a chance to clear his head and focus on what was important. His priority now was keeping her safe, even if she didn't want his help.

Her eyes narrowed and the muscles in her neck tightened. She wanted to tell him no. He could see it written all over her face. For a moment he saw her as she would have been at sixteen, seventeen, eighteen. Hell on wheels. Ready to kick ass and take names. The world had been hers. Every door had been opened to her. She could have done anything, been anything, been anyone she wanted.

And he wondered why she'd chosen this life instead.

What about it appealed to her? What about it made her feel safe?

Because that was really the question. At least, the only important one as far as he was concerned. He'd spent years defending his country. His business now centered on protecting those who couldn't protect themselves. And while he knew in his head that Anne was one tough cookie and could probably handle anything thrown her way...he had the sudden urge to surround her in Bubble Wrap and make sure no one ever hurt her.

"Fine. I'll be down in twenty minutes. Try not to burn the place to the ground." She muttered under her breath, "That would just be the perfect end to this day."

She was halfway up the stairs when she turned back to him. He could just see the toe of one of her ridiculous heels peeking out from the hem of her tailored suit pants.

"Oh, and just so we're clear. You might want to think twice about taking on an assignment that's doomed to failure before you've begun. I don't care what happens. I'm not going to Mother's."

PETER WATCHED as the man slipped out of the house and headed toward his car. He'd been surprised to see Blake Mitchell drive into the parking lot just as Annemarie had flown out of the house.

He wondered briefly why the other man was here but decided it didn't matter.

What did was that Anne was alone now and part of him wanted to slip back inside. To watch her. It would have been easy but would accomplish nothing, so he suppressed the urge and instead let his gaze wander across the redbrick facade of her town house, wondering what she was doing. Was she scared? Was she crying? Had his little stunt made her break down and sob?

He'd seen her face as she'd run from the town house, upset and fearful. There was something so satisfying about knowing exactly how to manipulate her.

He'd learned from the best and had no compunctions about putting his lessons to good use. No longer the insignificant, shy boy who had spent years living on the fringes, he'd come a long way from where he'd started as the stray Marie Prescott had reluctantly taken in out of a sense of duty.

He only wished he could have come to Anne's rescue instead of Mitchell. His hands fisted in anger.

He'd wanted to comfort her in her time of need.

But he couldn't. She had no idea he was here. And although she might not recognize him now, he couldn't take the chance. However, nothing prevented him from letting the fantasy take shape. The images played out in his mind. How she'd have run to him, her hands shaking as she'd buried her head in his neck and wrapped her fingers into the shirt over his chest. He'd have rubbed her back, up and down, as if she were the child from his memories.

The beautiful, wild, rebellious child with the flashing green eyes, tight pink mouth and silky blond hair. He'd watched her from the moment he'd gone to live on the Prescott estate. The perfect Prescott Princess.

She'd used her haughty tone to get whatever she'd wanted. She'd always had the most clothes, the most toys, the latest and greatest gadgets, and had never been satisfied. He'd watched her grow into the young woman who'd manipulated the world and people around her simply because she could.

He'd worshipped her from afar as she'd alternated between ignoring him completely and sneering at his awkward, shy existence. She'd delighted in proving that he didn't belong in her world. Her derision had crushed him.

She'd had everything and had thrown it all away. For what? Nothing! She was practically living in a hovel compared to where she could have been. Where she should have been.

If he'd been born into the Prescott family he definitely wouldn't have turned his back on all that offered.

He stared into her house, the gloom of dusk bringing shifting shadows with it. A light popped on in one of the upstairs windows, a glowing warmth that he begrudged her.

None of them deserved what they had. Most of all her.

She'd come running home, he'd make sure of that. And he'd be right there waiting for her.

He needed her. He hated her.

He wanted to hurt her, as she'd hurt him. And then he wanted to make it all better.

"WHERE DO YOU THINK you're going?"

Anne bit back a scream and whirled around to face Blake, fighting the urge to let the Louis Vuitton briefcase swing up and smack him.

She hadn't been sneaking. At least that's what she'd told herself as she'd tiptoed down the stairs and toward the front door. She was simply being polite to her guest. She hadn't wanted to disturb him, especially after he'd stayed up to deal with the lab tech the officer had sent over.

She also hadn't wanted him to trail behind her like a puppy dog all day. She didn't think she could take it. She'd slept like hell knowing he was down here, on her sofa, when he could have been in her bed.

"What does it look like? I'm going to work."

"Do you think that's wise?"

"If I'd like to pay my mortgage it is."

"Don't you have a rather sizable trust fund?"

Frustration rose inside her. She could feel the heat of the emotion bubbling in her stomach and spreading like acid through the rest of her body.

"Yes, I have a trust fund. A trust fund I do not touch. I do not use it to pay my mortgage, to buy my clothes or to sail my yacht."

"You have a yacht?"

It was all she could do not to stamp her feet on the floor and scream. Not a pleasant sensation, especially since she'd last experienced it when she was five, and had learned that temper tantrums only made her mother's cold attitude more frigid.

"No," she bit out through clenched teeth. "I do not have a yacht. It doesn't fit in my storage shed."

It took her a second to see the twinkle in his eyes and realize that he'd been teasing her. Somehow, that did not make her feel better.

Turning on her heel, she continued for the door. She expected him to stop her at any moment. To either insist on coming with her or try to persuade her to call in sick or quit. She was rather surprised when she'd made it all the way down the hall and had her hand on the doorknob and he still—

A telltale jingle sounded behind her, making her stomach knot. "You might need these."

Glancing over her shoulder, she watched as he shook her keys right in front of his face. And they were hers all right—the red rhinestone key chain that Karyn had given her last year glinted in the early-morning light.

She narrowed her eyes, taking him in and weighing his intent. How far would he go to keep her here?

"You aren't going to give those back, are you?"

A smile tugged at the corners of his lips. A twinkle lightened his dark eyes for the briefest moment before it was extinguished. "Nope."

He was enjoying this. Bastard.

Reaching into her bag, Anne pulled out her cell. "All right, I'll call a cab." She didn't even know the number for a cab company because it wasn't as if they littered the roads in Birmingham, but surely information could find her something.

She'd be late, but she'd get there.

"Or I could just drive you. Consider me your own personal chauffeur."

"I don't need a chauffeur. I need my car so I can get to work, preferably on time."

She still hadn't recovered from the tongue-lashing she'd gotten at work yesterday. She really didn't need to add fuel to the fire.

"Look, until we figure out what's going on or I'm convinced you aren't in danger, I'm not letting you out of this town house by yourself."

Anne scrunched her eyes shut, hoping for calm. The man was really starting to piss her off.

"The way I see it, you have two options. One, you let me take you to work, and when I'm satisfied you'll be safe there, I'll leave you alone and come back for you later. Two, I kidnap you and force you home to your mother."

She growled low in the back of her throat, frustration preventing the expletives she wanted to hurl at him from exiting. He wasn't a bastard; he was the lowest form of life she'd ever encountered—her mother's minion. And just like Marie, he thought he could run her life better than she could.

She reached for the doorknob again, but before she could touch it he was beside her, his hand gripping tight around her arm. "I can have you hog-tied in thirty seconds flat. You wanna try me?"

She looked into his eyes and hated him. No, she wanted to hate him. But she couldn't. Not when he was this close to her. Not when she could smell his spicy scent and feel the heat of him as he pressed his body against hers.

Her body, betraying, useless thing that it was, melted. Her muscles relaxed, the fight simply draining out of her. Her lips parted, she knew because the rush of air as it crossed her lips made them tingle. His eyes darkened, his pupils dilating, as he leaned closer.

His tongue licked out across his own open mouth. She wanted to chase it back inside. At least until he said, "Let me drive you to work," completely breaking the spell she'd been under.

Anne pushed against him, forcing space between their bodies.

She felt like a giant chess piece, maneuvered into a position not of her choosing.

She hated being manipulated.

She soothed her wounded pride with the knowledge that while he'd probably been trained in war tactics, she'd been trained in evasive maneuvers. She knew how to evade the paparazzi, how to evade her mother's notice…the list went on endlessly.

She'd become a little rusty lately, but she knew she could best him.

However at the moment, she didn't see that she had any choice but to go along peacefully. Reluctantly, she said, "Fine. Come with me."

6

ANNE JUMPED from the car, not waiting for Blake to follow. The car ride had been silent. She hadn't had anything to say to him and apparently he was intelligent enough to know she was ready to take his head off if he spoke to her.

He trailed one step behind her as they crossed the parking lot. She glanced over her shoulder once, expecting to find him ogling her ass, and was shocked to find his eyes scanning the rows of cars and open areas around them.

Jerking back around, she realized for the first time that Blake actually thought she was in danger. Up until this point part of her had assumed he was hanging around because he was hoping for a repeat performance.

He honestly believed she was in trouble.

Her heart fluttered for just a second. No. No. She wasn't in any real danger. This was all just coincidence and her mother's fancy footwork. In a day or two, when nothing else had happened, Blake would realize she was right and go away.

So why didn't that make her happy?

As they crossed into the lobby of the Walker head

office, Anne eyed the large gray room. One desk sat centered on the far wall between two key-card protected doors. They led to different areas of the company, Production and the executive offices. She would enter to the right.

Margret, the pretty redhead who sat behind the desk greeted her by name. "Good Morning, Ms. Sobel."

Anne stopped as a plan formed in her mind. Pulling up beside the desk, she leaned over the white wooden surface so that the other woman would be the only one to hear her words. "Margret, can you do me a favor?"

"Sure."

Glancing over her shoulder, she realized that Blake had stopped several feet away, giving her the space she needed to put her plan into action. "See that guy standing about five steps behind me?"

"Yes, ma'am."

"Stall him."

"What?"

"Stall him. Ask him a question. Get his attention. Make him sign in as a guest. Just don't let him follow me through the door."

"But why? What's wrong?" Margret's eyes widened. "Is he bothering you?" Her hand went automatically to the white phone sitting on the desk beside her. "Do I need to call security?"

"No, no. He isn't a threat. He just doesn't need to follow me inside."

Margret's eyebrows beetled, but she nodded. "All right."

Heading to the door, Anne pulled out her key card and waited. "Sir? I need you to sign in here please."

Anne glanced over her shoulder, enjoying the look

of wariness that entered his eyes. He glanced her way, saying "Wait for me," before going over to the desk.

She swiped her card, grabbed the handle as soon as the telltale beep sounded and yanked it open. It was seconds from the time the door opened to the time she pulled it shut behind her, her words drifting through the ever-closing space. "Enjoy staring at bad art for eight hours."

She heard his growl of frustration and his hand as it slapped down on the surface of the just-closed door. She knew he'd be waiting there when she came out. Served him right for strong-arming her the way he had. Maybe cooling his heels in the lobby for the next several hours would do him some good.

Probably not.

She rode the elevator up to the twelfth floor, winding her way through the cubicles to her office, which was built into the corner of the far west wall. She'd only moved into it recently thanks to her promotion.

She was peeling off her jacket as she went, ready to sling it onto her visitor chair and get straight down to business. She still needed to go over every detail of that sales report and see if she could figure out where the mistake had come from.

The sight inside stopped her in midstride.

There were two men at her computer, one sitting in her chair, his fingers on her keyboard and another standing over him, arms crossed, staring at the screen.

She groaned silently. There went her morning. Whenever IT showed up it meant at least an hour of twiddling her thumbs. If Karyn hadn't left the company in order to spend more time with Chris on his latest media tour, Anne could have gone down the hall and talked to her best friend. Instead, she stepped into her office and prepared to settle into the visitor chair herself and wait them out. Maybe it wouldn't be long.

"You guys back again? IT was just here last week."

The one standing turned to look at her, frowning, his blue-gray eyes cold.

"When was that?"

Anne shrugged. "Tuesday, I think. Yeah, Tuesday, because I was in the middle of running a report and it screwed up my whole day. But the guy said he needed to do it right then so…"

In fact, she'd been running the sales report at the time. It was a massive program and took a while to collect the data. Maybe that's what had gone wrong. Maybe it had been corrupted by something the IT guy had done.

"No one from IT has been scheduled to work on your system since it was moved."

"But…he was here."

"I'm head of IT. I'd know if one of my guys had been up here. I have the maintenance records for your system right here." He waved a file that she hadn't seen tucked to the far side of his body.

"We're going to be a while. Mr. Walker would like to see you, though."

"Okay." Anne didn't understand what was going on but surely the guy was mistaken. The IT guy's visit just hadn't been logged into her maintenance records, that was all.

With a shrug, she walked back out of her office, heading for the elevators and her trip up to the thirteenth floor. The doors opened onto pleasant office space, warm blues and greens decorating the walls. Mr. Walker's assistant glanced up from her computer screen, reached over for an intercom and announced that she was there. "Go on in. He's expecting you."

Anne walked to a double-doored office at the end of the hallway and pushed inside. The space was nice, not antiseptic and devoid of life but not too sumptuous and overbearing. It was comfortable. There were papers scattered across the desk. Mr. Walker was no figurehead owner—he worked hard and always had. She'd admired that about the man from the moment they'd met.

"Anne. Have a seat." She slipped into the waiting chair, not liking the hard expression on his face as she did. She'd always thought of him as a kind of mentor, the grandfather she'd never had. He'd been kind to her and encouraging about her role with Walker Technologies. He saw the value she brought to the company.

It had been a nice change from the constant emphasis on her flaws she'd received from her mother.

"If this is about that report…" Her words trailed off as he shook his head.

"I wish it were. Anne, you've been hiding something from us."

Her entire body flushed hot at his words. Damn it! This was really bad timing. Why did Mr. Walker have to find out about her secret now?

"How did you find out?"

"I received a phone call."

"Who?" Although she could guess. Damn Marie! The woman would stop at nothing to get what she wanted.

"I'm not sure. He wouldn't leave his name, but he had sufficient details of your job that I took what he said seriously. And after yesterday…"

Fine. So he knew who she was. She couldn't see what difference that made to anything. "It won't interfere with my ability to do my job, if that's your concern. I mean, no one else knows. Well, except Karyn, but she isn't here anymore so I can't see how that matters."

"Karyn? Karyn was involved in this as well?"

"Involved? No, I mean she knows who I really am, but she had nothing to do with why I left the family."

"The family? What are you talking about?"

Anne stared across at Mr. Walker. "I'm talking about being a Prescott. Annemarie Prescott. Isn't that what you're talking about?"

Mr. Walker slowly shook his head. "No. I'm talking about the accusation someone has made that you're a corporate spy. A perfect setup actually. As VP of marketing you have details about our new products long before they reach market. You have to, in order to do your job." His words were low, his eyes trained onto the center of his desk, almost as if he was explaining it to himself.

"But I've only had the job for a month."

"True, but you've had access to that kind of information for years, although I'll admit that no information has been leaked before now. At least, not that I'm aware of. What I don't understand is, why now?"

Sadness and disappointment entered his eyes as he finally looked at her again. That more than anything made her realize this was real. And that same feeling, the one of inadequacy that she'd fought her entire life, flared up inside her chest. She absolutely hated it.

"Was it money?"

"No! I don't need money. I have a damn trust fund." She was yelling. She realized somewhere in the back of her brain that it probably wasn't the best way to respond to the situation but she couldn't seem to stop herself. "I'm not spying on this company, Mr. Walker."

His eyes drifted back down to the top of his desk.

"Well, IT is looking at your computer now. They tell me it will likely take several days to do a complete audit. In the meantime, I think it would be best if you took a leave of absence until this can be resolved."

What could she say? She couldn't exactly refuse. He wasn't giving her that choice. Acid began to bubble up inside her stomach, a hot, burning pit of despair that she hadn't felt in a very long time. She wondered if an ulcer could refire in the space of seconds.

She lowered her voice, modulating it to something close to normal. "If you think that's best."

He glanced up at her for a moment before looking away again. "Security will escort you to your desk where you can collect any personal belongings you'll need."

She walked out of the office to find two suit-clad men she'd never seen before waiting for her. They were broad-shouldered and their faces held identical expressions of indifference. What did they expect she'd do?

What the hell had just happened?

BLAKE UNCROSSED his legs again, trying to find a comfortable position in the uncomfortable chair. He'd been staring at the same gray-tinted wall for the past hour and he thought if he had to do it for another seven or eight he might kill someone…namely one Anne Sobel.

He glanced at the artwork on the walls—she'd been right. It was bad—and then at the redhead behind the desk. He'd spoken to the woman almost immediately after the door had slammed behind Anne's back. She hadn't budged. He had to hand it to her. She might look like an insignificant piece of fluff but she had a spine.

The one saving grace was that he really didn't think Anne was in any danger inside the building. Especially if his inability to gain access was any indication. He eyed the access panel again from his seat. If he had a couple of tools and five minutes alone, he could easily get inside. But that was why the redhead was posted outside the door.

So far, he hadn't seen her leave, even to visit the ladies' room.

Blake shifted again when the telltale sound of a click at the far door sounded. He glanced up out of habit, cataloguing his space for threats.

But no threat walked through the door. Instead, it was Anne and she was not alone.

Two men he immediately identified as security marched on either side of her, half a step behind so they could react to anything she might do. He took two seconds to appreciate that whatever else they had going on, Walker Technologies had security covered, before he focused on Anne.

She wasn't happy, but considering there were only a few reasons for security to escort you out, he could understand that.

"What happened?" he asked, moving toward them as the trio crossed the lobby. Before Anne could open her mouth, the guard on the left stepped forward to block her. "Who are you?"

He gave the guy a lazy once-over just to show him that he wasn't intimidated by the nice suit, the hard voice and the laser stare.

"Her bodyguard."

The two men flanking Anne exchanged glances. Their expressions never changed, but they seemed to have some telepathic communication that no one else was in on.

The one who'd stepped forward said, "Then she's all yours. Mr. Walker will call you when he knows something, Ms. Sobel." And then with a precision that told Blake they were definitely ex-military, the two turned on their heels and walked back through the door they'd just exited.

Blake turned his focus back to Anne. Her skin was flushed and her eyes glowed as if they were lit from a fire within. Or maybe that was the sheen of unshed tears.

"What happened?"

"I was fired." Anne stalked toward the exit, not waiting for him to follow. "Well, put on administrative leave but I guarantee I won't be walking back through these doors again."

Her strides were long, eating up the ground as they headed for the car at the far side of the parking lot. "Why?"

"Apparently, they got a tip that I'm some kind of spy." She turned to glare at him, pinning him with her gaze. Anger was definitely winning, which was probably a good thing because he didn't think he could take seeing her in tears.

The urge to wrap her in his arms and promise her that everything would be okay suddenly warred with an unholy urge to march back into the building and crack whoever's head he came to first, starting with Tweedledee and Tweedledum and ending with Mr. Walker.

"Can you believe they think I'm selling company secrets? I've worked for that man for six years. I've stayed late, come in early, done anything and everything they've ever asked me to do." She turned on her heel and began stalking again, muttering "spy" beneath her breath.

At the moment, he believed she was capable of anything she wanted. But he knew that she wouldn't sell out Walker Technologies. She was loyal, one of the most loyal people he'd ever met. She was one-hundred percent devoted to his sister, to the point of putting herself in unpleasant situations just to make Karyn happy.

"Damn, damn, damn!" She stopped again, spinning. "You had better not tell Marie about this. God!" She tilted her head back and stared up at the sky as if praying for mercy...or asking for strength. "If she finds out, she'll have the jet here so fast your head will spin. I've held her off for months with the argument that I have a job I can't leave."

Her gaze fell from the sky, locking with his. "I don't have that anymore, do I?"

She stomped off again. Blake thought briefly of trying to calm her temper but decided it was safest to let it run its course. So far, she hadn't threatened herself or any innocent bystanders.

"I know she's responsible. I don't know how she did it, but I have no doubt Marie Prescott's hand is in this somehow."

She was delusional. Clearly.

He must have made a sound of protest because, just as they reached the car, she turned to him again, this time stopping short enough so their bodies were centimeters apart.

"Don't you dare doubt it. You might think I've gone off the deep end but you aren't familiar with Marie's tactics. She's a Prescott and she'll stop at nothing to get what she wants. And she wants me home. I have no idea why. Why now? But I gave her an obstacle and she found a way around it. A way that most likely involved breaking and entering, but then what's a little criminal activity between family members?"

He waited silently as air blew in and out of her lungs.

Her chest rose and fell with the force of her anger and her eyes blazed. But he could see the disappointment and fear that also lingered there.

Without thought he reached for her, wanting to give her whatever solace he could. But she turned from him before he could touch her, the heel of one of her fancy shoes catching in a crack. He watched as she pitched forward, her face heading straight for asphalt.

7

HER FIRST THOUGHT as the heel of her shoe stuck in the crack was, *not the Manolos!* Her body pitched, her foot refusing to move when it should. She could feel her center of gravity shifting, her weight moving forward, the pavement getting closer and closer.

Warm hands reached out and stopped her. She hung in midair, her body suspended between disaster and Blake. Slowly, he rolled her around, pulling her in and bringing her upright and into his chest. Her hands fisted in his shirt, grabbing handfuls of him, even if she hadn't wanted them.

His body was warm and hard…solid in a way nothing else in her life ever had been. It was wrong. This was wrong. She didn't want this and should move away.

But she didn't.

Gently, Blake covered her hands with his own and unfurled her fingers. He dropped to his knee at her feet in the parking lot. The expression on her face must have been priceless for anyone who'd cared to watch.

His palm slid around her foot, cradling her heel in one hand. His other ran up the inside leg of her pants to cup her calf. There should have been nothing sexy in that, but heat, low and hard, started simmering in her center.

He wiggled the back of her shoe, steadying her with the support of his hand as he worked the heel out of the pavement. A smile touched his lips, showing satisfaction at what he'd done for her.

A cool rush of air followed him as he slowly stood up. His body brushed against hers, setting off alarm bells and chain lightning across her skin.

She thought he was going to kiss her, watched as his eyes darkened in the same way they'd done that first night as he'd crossed the dance floor toward her. Her lips fell open, inviting him in. He moved closer. She could feel his breath across her temple and the crackle of awareness from his skin.

Instead he reached between them, lifting the keys from her lax fingers. "I think I should drive."

He walked away, leaving her breathless and unsatisfied. He hadn't even touched her and her sex throbbed with the ache of wanting him.

How could he do that to her? How could he tear through ten years of walls and barricades and rip into the wanton hedonist she used to be?

Fighting the urge to scream, she followed behind him. She had other things she should be worrying about. Big things. Like how she was going to pay her electric bill, not to mention the credit card bill for her last splurge in Atlanta. She had some savings but if this dragged on...

No one would hire her with this cloud of suspicion hanging over her head. Her anger heated again, momentarily subverted by the promise of Blake and the temptation of his mouth. She was going to kill her mother.

"IT'S BEEN twenty-four hours. She still isn't leaving. You must do something more."

Peter listened to the voice at the other end of the phone. Full of authority yet somehow frail. Maybe it was simply the incongruous picture in his head that went along with the voice.

Only he had been allowed to see the vulnerability as it had crept into Marie Prescott's world. Over the past few months it had gotten more and more difficult to keep the truth hidden. The moment she'd begun to lose her hair and had a rather large radiation cross tattooed on her forehead, they'd both had to get creative. Marie had taken the opportunity to pull out the biggest jewel she owned—a sapphire—and hung it from a turban to hide the cross. She'd never been eccentric before but they'd both decided she could get away with it now. Her air of authority and entitlement meant no one questioned her when she made a bold move.

They both knew she was running out of time.

Marie had sent him to bring her precious daughter home. Annemarie was her only hope for the future of her company and family. Ever subservient, Peter had agreed. Marie had no need to know he'd wanted the same thing, that he had his own agenda at work.

He'd thought taking away Annemarie's sense of security and her job would send her racing back to the safety of the family. Apparently she was stronger than he'd realized.

It was time to turn the screws and really impress upon her the danger she was in. The fact that Mitchell was lurking around would make things difficult—the man specialized in security. He had no idea why Mitchell had shown up now. Peter realized they'd had a fling at the wedding but he'd assumed it was over since he hadn't seen the man around her before now.

"I'll take care of it, Marie. Don't I always?"

There was no response or acknowledgement as the line went dead. Not that he'd expect any appreciation when he'd never gotten a thank-you before.

Marie would die soon. And when she did, he was poised to take everything he'd ever wanted.

When it was all over, he'd finally be a member of the family who'd taken him in and shunned him at the same time. He'd have access to their fortune, their fame, the doors that opened with just their name. He'd have everything they'd held over his head and taunted him with. And they'd have nothing.

He'd enjoy seeing a resurgence of Annemarie's fear. The one downside to getting her fired had been seeing anger replace the lingering doubt his break-in had left her with. He loved knowing that his actions had influence over her emotions, but he preferred to see her vulnerable.

He was pulling her strings and she didn't even know it. He couldn't help the smile of pure joy that spread across his face.

"REMIND ME again why we're doing this."

Blake stared around him at the line of high-end boutiques. Expensive designer labels glared back. He should probably recognize several of the names. He didn't and frankly couldn't care less. But Anne had stomped down the stairs this morning, announcing, "I'm leaving for a while. You can come if you want but you'd better get ready fast or I'm going without you."

She'd been in a mood and he hadn't wanted to make it worse. Actually, she'd been in a mood since they'd left her office parking lot yesterday. He didn't blame her, but being her punching bag was getting old fast. He wasn't used to sitting still, or taking shit from anyone, and it was really starting to grate on him.

Of course, he probably hadn't helped the situation by immediately suggesting they head for New York. Yeah, not the smartest idea he'd ever had. She'd ripped him a good one over that.

He had to admit that so far there hadn't been any more evidence that she was in danger. He was almost willing to concede that her theory of unconnected coincidence was just as likely as Marie's theory of a stalker. However, that didn't mean he was going to take a chance with her life testing out the theory. Especially when one meant she was safe and the other meant she could end up hurt or dead.

No way was he going to let that happen. No way was he going to let another woman come to harm on his watch. Even if it meant continuing to rile her with his presence.

It didn't help that every moment he spent with her, hearing her, seeing her, touching her, and not being able to have her, just made him burn more. Listening to the creak of the floor beneath her feet at midnight and imagining her in a short little slip of silk and lace, studying her smooth curves as she moved through her home…it was like stoking the dying coals of a fire and not expecting new flames to erupt.

The tension had become so thick he could taste it. He'd spent the past twenty-four hours in a constant state of semi-erection just waiting for the smallest glimpse of her skin or the slightest catch of her breath to push him toward full-fledged, growling need.

Her couch had become incredibly uncomfortable,

especially knowing that if he'd walked up those stairs not only would he find the comfort of a bed but the welcome relief of her body. Not exactly conducive to a restful sleep. But she hadn't given him any indication that his touch would be welcome.

So frankly, he wasn't in the best of moods, either.

"I told you. I needed to get out of the house for a little while. The walls were closing in."

The pointed glance she threw over her shoulder clearly indicated what she wanted to get away from was him. Too bad.

He wandered behind her, asking questions, annoying ones. Poking fun at her confusing need for high-end fashion products, enjoying her exasperated looks and the cute way her nose wrinkled when he frustrated her.

Finally, after a particularly snide comment, she said, "Forget it. Let's go."

He'd watched as she'd looked through a legion of handbags, stroking the leather as if it were ermine or silk. She must have tried on fifty pair of shoes. Heels—low, high and break your neck. Flats, sandals, anything and everything. She'd sprayed perfume after perfume and tried on designer suit after designer suit.

But she hadn't bought a thing.

He'd expected to walk out of there like a camel set for months in the desert.

Whatever. Shrugging, he followed behind her, heading for the parking lot.

While her tiny red sports car didn't exactly stick out in the lot of expensive cars, it was hard to miss. He hadn't thought about it until now though, but the car didn't quite match the woman he was getting to know. While her blond-bombshell exterior, expensive clothes, perfectly applied makeup and hot car all screamed sex, she hadn't exactly turned out to be the you're willing, I'm able, screw-me-senseless type.

Though she'd been a tigress in bed, and any person who'd read the headlines when she was younger knew she'd had plenty of experience, he was coming to realize she very rarely gave that passionate side free rein. At least not anymore. Oh, it poked through on occasion, but for the most part it was as if she'd surgically removed those impulses from her personality.

He mused as they crossed the lot, unable to stop himself from watching the sway of her hips and the tight little curve of her ass.

God, he wanted that tigress in his bed again.

Anne had just rounded the hood of her car, keys in hand, when a pop shot through the air and his heart leaped to his throat. He knew that sound. Had heard it more times than he ever wanted to count.

Just as he yelled at her to get down, the back window of the car exploded in a shower of glass shards. Pulling his gun from its holster, he ran to her side, pushing her to the ground in front of the car and placing his body between hers and the direction the bullet had come from.

"Shit."

His fault. If he'd been paying attention to everything around them instead of staring at her ass this never would have happened.

He waited for more bullets to fly, for more pops and more explosions, but none came. After several tense minutes, Blake looked at Anne. "Call nine-one-one."

She nodded, her green eyes wide, full of shock, fear and a despair that made his chest ache. He didn't have time for that now, though. His first priority was her safety.

Pulling his feet beneath him in a crouch, Blake stuck his head around the corner of the front bumper. When nothing jumped out at him, he bunched his muscles up and prepared to dash for the car beside them.

With a squeak of protest, Anne reached out for him.

Shaking his head, he stared into her eyes for a second. "I'll be right back."

Using the other cars in the lot for cover, Blake made his way across to a small half wall that surrounded the area. A rich red brick, it was meant to show the affluence of the people who shopped here. It had also provided the perfect cover for the sniper who'd tried to kill Anne.

Although, whoever it was couldn't have been a very good shot. Marksmanship hadn't been his forte, but even he could have made a clean shot from this far away.

Somehow, that did not make him feel better. In fact, it made his stomach churn with a sick sludge of acid and guilt.

As he reached the wall, he quickly stuck his head over before pulling it back. After he was certain no bullets would come flying, he took a longer look. Just as he'd suspected—nothing. Whoever had been here was long gone.

He made his way back across the parking lot to Anne. The sour mix still in his stomach finally began to ease as he saw her sitting there on the pavement. Her back was pressed to the bumper of her car, her knees drawn tight to her chest, her cell phone gripped in her hand.

"Anne?"

She looked up at him, her eyes glassy and faraway. "They should be here in just a minute."

Sitting down on the hard, cold asphalt beside her,

Blake gathered her into his lap. Her body was shaking; he could feel the quivers as they passed up and down her spine. He hadn't realized until he'd touched her. God, she was a strong little thing, holding her reactions and emotions in.

He was startled for a second when she turned her body so that she could bury her head in his chest. Her hands wrapped around the back of his neck, her fingers ice-cold both from the winter weather and shock.

He tightened his arms around her back and rocked as if to push up. Her sound of protest vibrating against his chest stopped him.

"You're cold. Let me take you inside."

"I'm fine. I don't want to move."

Considering someone had just shot at her, her reluctance to leave their hiding place until the police came was understandable.

Settling back down, he pulled her closer and tried to wrap his body around her as much as possible. At least the shaking had stopped.

Wisps of blond hair tickled his face and he almost yelped as her cold nose found the warm crook of his neck. Her fingers curled into his skin and she shifted so that she could get closer.

Her breath was warm on his skin but her lips were warmer. He groaned as they touched his neck. Need stirred hard and quick in his blood.

Wrong place. Wrong time. It was the story of their relationship. But that didn't seem to stop him from wanting her.

She pulled back so that her eyes met his. They were darker than normal. He couldn't read anything there though, anything aside from the same desire that was slipping through him. Maybe he didn't want to see anything else.

"Kiss me."

Her words were soft but her lips on his were not. She didn't even wait for him to do as she asked; instead she swooped in and took what she wanted.

There was heat and emotion and desire and the bitter aftertaste of fear. He didn't want her to be scared. He didn't want fear to be what drove her to him. He wanted her in his arms because she wanted him with the same driving need that he felt. He wanted her there because she couldn't forget about him…just as he hadn't been able to forget about her.

But for now he'd take this. Because they both needed it. She required a moment of safety and heat, he a moment to prove that she was okay. That he hadn't failed to protect her.

The ground was uncomfortable. The car at his back was hard. But Anne was soft and pliant and sweet. Her lips moved against his. Her tongue stroked inside his mouth. Her hands held him tight. He'd have endured a bed of nails if it meant kissing, touching and tasting her again.

Breathless, she pulled back and stared up into his face. He gazed down at her, realizing in that moment that this woman had come to mean something to him. He cared about her.

And that scared the hell out of him.

For years his whole existence had centered around protecting people. First with Special Forces and now as he designed and implemented security systems like the one at Walker Technologies. Always before, professional pride had driven him to do his job well. Now, there was more.

With Anne it wasn't just a job. It was personal. And there was no way he'd be taking Marie's money.

But what if he couldn't keep her safe? The thought had fear coursing through him, tightening his skin as if it were suddenly too small to fit his body. If he failed... if something happened to her...

He wouldn't be able to live with himself.

"You're going home." He wasn't going to take no for an answer.

He'd drag her kicking and screaming if he had to, but the family compound was the safest place for her, and taking a chance with her life because she wanted to dig her heels in and be stubborn was no longer an option.

To his surprise she nodded instead of protesting. Her eyes were still glazed over with desire, her lips moist and dark pink from his kisses.

And he knew this couldn't happen again. She'd almost gotten killed because he'd been distracted. Even knowing that, he hadn't stopped to think twice before taking her mouth and plunging them both into a sea of desire. A blinding sea.

When she was in his arms he couldn't focus on anything else. So she couldn't be in his arms. Not while she was in danger.

8

ANNE STIRRED restlessly in her seat. She'd sprung for first-class tickets.... Rather, her mother had sprung for first-class tickets. If she was going home, the woman was going to pay her way.

However, despite the increased space between her and Blake, she still felt uneasy.

Part of what had her on edge was certainly the woman who waited for her at the other end of this flight. She hadn't seen her mother in ten years. And that wasn't nearly long enough.

But the man beside her could at least claim partial responsibility for her restlessness. Was it just her imagination or had the recirculated air begun to smell entirely of him? It was as if she couldn't get away, no matter how far she shifted.

"What should I expect?"

They were almost the first words he'd spoken to her in the past twelve hours. That was precisely how long it had taken him to arrange this little trip down memory lane, including a call to Karyn to let her know they'd be gone for a while. Blake had agreed to tell his sister only that they were leaving and not mention the shooting or the break-in. Neither of them wanted to worry Karyn any more than necessary. Anne supposed there was no hope of hiding her one-night transgression from her best friend now, either.

She was puzzled by his change in attitude. He'd gone from hot and heavy to cold and distant in the space of a heartbeat. She didn't understand why.

Not that she wanted him pawing at her or anything… or at least not on the plane in front of witnesses, but the about-face had startled her. He was no longer the warm, teasing man who'd been sleeping on her couch for the past few nights.

He was all business.

She resented that. She was nervous and fidgety and he was…bored. Her mind kept replaying the kiss they'd shared and he was acting as if it had never happened.

"What do you mean?"

"Exactly what I asked. What should I expect? Anyone here who might give you—us—problems?"

"Absolutely." She laughed bitterly. "But not the way you're thinking."

He stared at her with an infinite amount of patience, which she envied, waiting for her to elaborate. She would have but she didn't really know how to without revealing more of herself to him than she wanted.

Finally, she settled for, "Somehow I don't think your military training prepared you for my mother. Can your flak jackets stop barbed tongues and knife-edged comments?"

His mouth pulled into a frown and his chocolate eyes turned opaque. She didn't like that. She much preferred them clear and deep—filled with lust for her. God, she was a glutton for punishment.

"I've spoken to your mother."

"Sure. On the phone. There was the buffer of distance. Trust me, in person her level of charm is somewhere between Satan and a snake. You will do nothing right. You are below her notice."

"Why do you hate her so much?"

The genuine bafflement in his voice didn't really surprise her. She'd met Blake's family. They were the Norman Rockwell of normal. Loving, joking, teasing... Certainly, they weren't perfect, and they'd had their own share of pain and anguish, but he could never understand the level of unhappiness, disappointment and loneliness that had been the fabric of her life.

She didn't want him to understand. It would be too awkward for her if he knew the depth of the pit she'd finally crawled out of. The true embarrassment was that the pit hadn't been entirely dug by her mother. She'd certainly had a hand in orchestrating her own destruction. What was worse was that she'd pulled her brother down with her and never realized—or cared—that she was doing it.

He'd been the one to pay the ultimate price. She found solace in the fact that because of his actions she'd gotten away. She thought Michael would have liked that.

She sighed. "There are too many reasons to count."

"Name one."

"She killed my brother."

The answer was unexpected even as it flew from her mouth. It was a simplified version of the truth that didn't account for her own involvement that night. Anne would never forgive herself for what had happened. For the fact that when Michael had finally taken her advice and told their mother he was gay, and it had blown up in his face, she hadn't been there to comfort and help him.

She'd left him alone, desperate and emotional enough to kill himself.

While she'd gone out to party.

She'd lost everything that night. The only person who'd ever given a shit about her. She'd been completely wrapped up in her own shallow existence and oblivious to her brother's pain. The pain he hadn't been strong enough to shoulder by himself.

"Your mother is powerful but I have a hard time believing she can get away with murder."

A sick smile twisted her lips. "You'd be surprised what she can get away with. But no, she didn't put the rope around Michael's neck. However, she absolutely helped tie the knot."

Just as Anne had. It had taken her years to realize the guilt would never go away. That there was nothing she could do to correct the situation. Her brother was dead and always would be. It was an irreversible action none of them could take back.

The difference was her cold and heartless mother didn't seem to want to.

The one time they'd talked about it, she'd been hard and bitter. She'd been angry with Michael. She hadn't recognized or admitted her part in the situation at all. And nothing Marie had said since convinced Anne she'd had a change of heart.

Until she did, Anne would hate her.

Her gaze traveled slowly across Blake's face. His expression was distant. Focused. Unlike the heated, passionate man he'd been the night they'd met, unlike the playful and irritating man he'd been the past couple days.

He was different. But maybe that was good.

She didn't like the person she became around her

mother. Old habits died hard and somehow her mother's caustic and sarcastic outlook on life pulled against the hard-won barriers she'd erected over the years.

Part of her was afraid Blake wouldn't like the way she was around Marie, either, that he'd no longer see her as a capable, independent woman, but as the party girl she'd once been. She feared those old coping mechanisms— the need for release, revenge and freedom—would bear down on her and leak out in an inappropriate or unhealthy manner. They always had before. The only surefire way she'd found to stop the knee-jerk reactions was to stay out of her mother's sphere.

She already wondered if her one night with Blake had been the first step on the slippery slope back to bad, self-destructive decisions. Habits that had the potential to destroy much more than the safe and simple life she'd built for herself. She'd spent the past several days fighting urges so strong they scared her. What would happen when she put that old life and the only man to tempt her to sin again together?

Water and oil?

Probably more like gunpowder and a match.

She hoped she was strong enough to deal with both her mother and the attraction she felt for Blake at the same time.

The sound of hydraulics whined through the plane as the landing gear dropped. She was about to find out.

BLAKE WATCHED Anne carefully. He didn't like what he saw. She was tense enough to pop a muscle.

He knew there was more to the story she'd told him on the plane—more that she wasn't ready to share. In his line of work, he'd learned that there truly were two sides to every story. He wondered how Marie's version of Anne's life and her brother's suicide would differ.

Of course he believed Anne. She was in too much pain for there not to be true wounds behind the walls she'd built. But he wondered how much of her memory was colored by the rebellious party girl she'd been back then. She hadn't exactly been her mother's biggest fan.

Oh, he wasn't deluding himself. Marie Prescott was cold and calculating. But he doubted she was a murderer. Although he'd be the first to admit that people weren't always what they appeared. Hadn't he struggled for years with guilt over the fact that he'd introduced his sister to her rapist? A guy he'd thought was decent?

Certainly, he understood not everyone's upbringing had been as ideal as his own. But it wasn't as if Anne had been raised on the streets. Her family had given her every advantage under the sun.

However, he got a much better perspective when they walked from the baggage claim area into the hustling action of the curb outside the door.

A sleek black limo with dark tinted windows waited there—in a zone clearly marked No Parking. The security guard standing several feet away ignored the driver's flagrant disregard for the posted sign, his eyes drifting over the car almost as if it were invisible.

It bothered Blake—following rules had been ingrained in him from birth and reinforced by years of obeying orders. It bothered him more when the driver, an older gentleman dressed in a spotless black suit and white shirt, stood up from his location against a pillar and said, "Welcome home, Miss Annemarie."

The smile on the driver's face was at least friendly. And it actually surprised Blake when Anne dropped her bag onto the sidewalk, ran the five steps to the man, and threw her arms around his neck.

He'd never seen her that open with anyone. Maybe she was that way with Karyn and he hadn't been paying attention but he didn't think so.

"George. I can't believe you're here. I thought you would have retired long before now. You should have."

She pulled away, her hands still on his arms, and let her eyes travel lovingly across his face. Her smile was genuine, touching her eyes in a way that turned them a brilliant emerald.

The window in the back of the limo rolled down and a voice, crystal clear and demanding, rang from inside.

"Stop making a spectacle of yourself, Annemarie, and get inside this car."

The light in Anne's eyes died quickly, instantly smothered by dismay and surprise. The driver looked at her with sad, apologetic eyes before walking quickly away from her to pick up the abandoned bag from the sidewalk.

Anne's back stiffened as she took a long, deep breath. She fixed a smile on her face, this one a complete and utter lie, before she turned to the limo. She must have forgotten Blake was there because surprise cracked her facade for a fraction of a second.

She turned her attention to the other man. "George, can you get Mr. Mitchell's bag, as well, please?"

"Certainly."

Before Blake could protest, the other man gently extricated the overnight bag from his hand. It wasn't big and didn't hold very much. He hadn't packed for an extended stay when he'd set out for Anne's place. She'd assured him they'd get whatever he needed. Eyeing the limo, he had no doubt that was true.

Dropping both bags at his feet, George opened the car's door for them.

Blake waited for Anne. She slipped into the backseat, going all the way to the far side before turning to look back out the still-open door at him.

"Mother, this is Blake Mitchell. Although I understand you've hired him, I doubt that you've met him." The gaze she leveled at her mother spoke volumes. "He'll be joining us."

Blake ducked his head and entered the car, his eyes staying on Anne's as he settled into his seat. The door shut immediately behind him and for a second he fought the memories of the slamming cell door. He hadn't thought about those three months of lost freedom in a very long time.

Dragging his gaze from Anne, he finally looked at the woman sitting across from them.

She wasn't as old as he'd imagined her. He'd guess somewhere in her late fifties but he'd give her early sixties based on the potential for plastic surgery alone. Her face was flawlessly made-up, though it was on the thin side. Her head was covered by a swath of fabric that exactly matched the dark blue of the power suit she wore. But what caught his attention and held it for several seconds was the huge teardrop sapphire that hung to the center of her forehead.

For a second he wondered if it was real. He shook his head. Of course it was real. And it could probably have fed a third world country for a year. It was garish and ostentatious and somehow did not fit Marie Prescott's image and mannerisms.

Finally pulling his gaze away, he forced himself to

look her in the eye. Her expression was cold, her mouth a straight, disapproving line. She evaluated him from head to toe and clearly found him lacking. He'd never experienced that. Mothers loved him.

Her eyes narrowed to slits. "It took you long enough."

She was...shocked. Her mother looked like hell, although the frailty didn't seem to affect her tongue. Guilt, something she was getting pretty darn tired of feeling, rushed over her. Her mother really was sick.

She wondered what Marie had. By the looks of her it was pretty serious.

Anne watched as Marie walked ahead of her. It was even more apparent here, outside the dark confines of the car, that Marie's illness was ravaging her body. She took in the halting way her mother walked. She noticed the way George helped her from the car and kept pace one step behind her, with his hand ready for quick action. The labored breaths that simply making her way up the sweeping front stairs had caused.

Still, Marie maintained her formidable facade. She refused to accept any help or show any overt sign of weakness. There was no mistaking she was still the same driven woman she'd always been.

One other thing hadn't changed. The sheer number of people who seemed to live at the estate for no discernible reason.

Her Aunt Kitty—Kathy was her real name but no one had called her that since her days at prep school almost forty years ago. Kitty looked up at her from the corner of the living room sofa. Her eyes were glassy, vacant. Anne wondered what the drug of choice was these days. When she'd been home it had been alcohol and pain pills. Somehow she thought her aunt had moved on to stronger stuff. Probably with her mother's money, since Kitty had none left of her own.

Her cousins—Max and Mark, twins—sat across from their mother, their heads close together, in a deep conversation that looked rather stiff and heated. For a split second she wished she could hear what they'd been discussing, but as her mother swept into the room they abruptly shut their mouths and turned to face her.

Peter Berg, the orphaned son of her mother's good friend sat off to the side by himself. For as long as she could remember he'd been a silent member of the household. He'd floated somewhere in between—not a member of the family but not a part of the staff, either. For the most part, Anne had ignored his presence. They hadn't traveled in the same circles, although they had been fairly close in age. She wasn't really surprised to find him still here after so many years—her mother liked to keep people close, where she could control them.

There were several others in the room, people she'd never met. Or rather, people she didn't remember meeting. If they were friends of the twins, she'd probably met them at some club or other. She had some pretty big memory gaps from that time period.

"Annemarie is home to take her rightful place."

Her mother was making a bold statement—Anne was the prodigal daughter…the one who truly belonged here. And Anne couldn't help but notice the undercurrents of tension running through the people around her.

Obviously, she'd known her cousins—and probably her aunt, since she'd do whatever her precious boys told her—would be less than enthusiastic about her return. She was certain they'd long hoped to gain control of the company in order to tap directly into the family fortune instead of begging for scraps.

She didn't care what the others in the room thought.

Anne stopped beside her mother, a tight smile on her face. No sense in starting off on a bad foot for no reason.

She was slightly surprised when Blake stepped up beside her, his hand resting lightly at the center of her back. She wasn't sure if the gesture was a sign of claim to the other men in the room or a show of solidarity. She wasn't sure which one she would have preferred. Maybe both if she was being honest with herself.

"Oh, and Blake Mitchell. A friend."

The way her mother twisted the last word had Anne's eyes narrowing. But she refused to turn her head and look at her mother. Refused to acknowledge the implication and disapproval Marie had put into that single word.

George came up behind them, saving them all from the increasing tension and displeasure that seemed to swell to fill the space.

"Miss Annemarie, I've placed you in the west wing of the house. Mr. Mitchell is in the suite opposite yours."

She turned briefly, for some reason reluctant to take her eyes from the crowd of people staring at her—almost as if she expected them to attack the moment she turned her back. "Thank you, George."

BLAKE SPRAWLED in the chair opposite her bed, watching as she took her clothes from the suitcase and hung them up in the open closet. A maid had materialized shortly after they'd arrived and offered to do the task for her. Anne had refused.

He had no doubt that someone was touching all his

shirts, jeans and underwear and putting them into a drawer. It bothered him. But not nearly as much as leaving Anne here alone. He couldn't put his finger on it, but he was uneasy, had been since they'd slid into the limo.

Something here wasn't right—the hairs at the back of his neck had been standing at attention for the past hour. It was an instinct he couldn't ignore.

He studied her as she moved with smooth and competent motions. He'd only known her for a little over a month, and already he could guess what her response would be if he suggested they leave. Especially considering what it had taken to get her here in the first place.

He'd thought she would be safer here. He was no longer certain of that. In fact, he was seriously fighting the urge to throw her over his shoulder and disappear with her to a place where he could protect her.

But he'd seen her reaction to the sight of her mother. The woman was seriously ill and despite the problems in their relationship, he knew Anne would never agree to leave her now. Especially considering she hadn't believed Marie when she'd told Anne she was sick.

She didn't want to be here any more than he did. And yet guilt and obligation would make her stay.

So he'd stay with her, make sure she was protected—physically and emotionally. He'd be her ally because it didn't appear she had very many. He'd stand by her side. And whatever happened, he would not get distracted again.

"You can go home if you want."

Her words were soft. Precise. And he heard the reluctance in them even if she didn't want him to. She wanted him to stay.

"I'm not leaving you alone."

"Alone?" She laughed, although there was no humor in the sound. "Hardly alone. There must be a dozen people in that room right now."

And none of them cared one whit what happened to her. In fact, he'd guess several of them would delight in seeing her hurt, in bruising her ego and position.

"I said I'd keep you safe."

"I thought that was the whole reason for coming here. To keep me locked behind the compound walls, a modern day Rapunzel."

"You hardly qualify as a helpless princess. Pampered, yes. Helpless, no."

This time the smile she gave him was genuine, if fleeting. "Either way, you've delivered me safely to the queen and can go now."

"I think I'll stick around...just to make sure she isn't really the evil witch."

Her mouth curved into a smile—a poor approximation of her normal, teasing, tempting smile, but it was better than nothing. Besides, for the first time since they'd boarded the plane, her shoulders relaxed a little, the stiffness melting slowly away.

He stood up from the chair, moving toward her before he'd even registered the intent to wrap her in his arms and hold her tight. He stopped himself midstride. Reaching for some knickknack off the dresser, he turned it over absently in his hands instead as he asked, "What is wrong with your aunt?"

"Drug of choice. Who knows what that is anymore?"

"And your cousins creep me out. They looked a little too involved with each other."

"Twins. I don't think they've ever been more than a room away from each other since they were born. They do everything together, go everywhere together. There was this rumor that they only have sex with women they agree on. And then they both have her, one after the other. I've seen some kinky shit and even I thought that was creepy. It's almost as if they share a brain."

She finished putting her clothes away and stood staring at the empty suitcase for several moments before moving it to the floor and taking its place under the bed. She sat facing him, her hands folded perfectly in her lap, her ankles crossed and tucked beneath her body.

He'd never seen her act this way—proper. She was strong and confident. She had no problems with flouting anything—including propriety—if she felt like it. There was something unnatural about the way she sat.

His brain immediately replaced the picture of her sitting there with another. Her hair ruffled and messy. Her eyes burning up at him. Her lips parted in invitation. The perfectly arranged bedspread crumpled into a ball at the end of the bed and their clothes tangled together with it. Her body, flushed pink with desire, writhing beneath him.

That was how she belonged. Sensual, loved, aroused.

Again, he ran a single finger down the smooth slope of her cheek. He convinced himself that this was okay. There was no danger here, behind the closed door of her bedroom. And all he was doing was offering her a moment of comfort. Nothing more. This was for her, not him.

She rubbed her face against the touch, closing her eyes in quiet appreciation. The burn in his belly quickly told him he'd miscalculated. He flipped his hand over and palmed her neck, letting it run down until his fingertips slipped beneath the open V of her sweater. He brushed over the bump of her collarbone and fought the urge to go lower.

A low-throated moan escaped her open lips.

He leaned in close, kneeling on the floor at her feet.

And then she opened her eyes. Yes, they were dazed and unfocused, bright with the same desire coursing through his body. But beneath that was a desperation and despair that stopped him cold.

He didn't want to be her anesthetic.

Surging to his feet, he pulled his hand from her body and took two steps back.

She watched him, heat turning into a hard shell of glittering green. For one brief moment he thought she might come after him, that knife-edged brightness slicing through his one moment of sanity and forcing him to accept his basest needs over his resolve to keep his hands off her for her own sake.

Instead, she blew out a breath, a steadying stream of air that seemed to calm everything inside her. Her lips thinned into a frown as she shifted on the bed, that prim and proper posture finally disappearing.

"Want to get out of here?" It seemed like the smartest idea, getting her as far away from a bed as humanly possible.

She lifted an eyebrow at him, the not-quite smile touching her lips again. "More than you know, but we can't. Dinner's in a little while, and if I don't show up Marie will rake me over the coals. And while that wouldn't have bothered me before, I find the desire to rile my mother that sustained me through my teenage years has suddenly deserted me." She looked up at him with sad eyes. "Great timing, huh?"

9

It HAD BEEN three days and she was going stark, raving mad. Three boring, tense and emotionally raw days. Anne stared at herself in the mirror, applying the last touches of makeup before she could head to the dining room for breakfast. She rolled her eyes. Full-on regalia for breakfast. Right about now she was longing for her usual Saturday ritual of yoga pants, Starbucks and nothing but sunscreen on her face.

She'd barely spoken to her mother, although the words said had been far from pleasant. Her cousins were acting very odd and frankly made her creep meter ping. Her aunt was so out of it as to be almost nonexistent.

And Blake. Sitting in the same room with him made her want to squirm, an activity Mother would have frowned upon. Prescotts were never affected by mundane things like desire. They were above being ruled by their emotions.

Bullshit.

She'd had enough. There'd been no sign of any danger. She'd spoken to her mother's doctor when he'd come to the house. There was nothing she could do here. Her mother was dying. Two days. Two weeks. Two years. No one knew. But considering the woman wouldn't take a tissue from her, much less allow any gestures of comfort, Anne could do nothing to help ease the situation.

Her presence was actually more likely to cause her mother stress, something the doctor had said probably wouldn't be wise.

Finally ready, Anne waited for Blake in the sitting room down the hall from their suites, and pulled him aside as he made his way toward the dining room for breakfast.

"I'm thinking about leaving tomorrow."

"I admit your family makes me uneasy, but I'm not sure that's a good idea."

"Why?"

Blake crossed his arms over his chest. "You're still in danger." She wondered if he was aware that he'd moved closer to the doorway, making it look as if she'd have to go through him if she wanted out of here.

"Nothing's happened in days."

"That's because you aren't at home, making yourself a target. You're safe here, which was the entire point of coming."

That might be the case, but the result was that she was going crazy from boredom, tension and emotions she didn't want to deal with.

"Look, I can't put my life on hold indefinitely. I need to get back. I have a job." She ignored his pointed glance. "And responsibilities. Prada needs me."

She was regretting boarding her cat at the vet's office, but at the time it had seemed the smart thing to do. Prada was prone to stress-related hissy fits and traveling always stressed her out. Now she was thinking at least an incident with her cat would have provided some welcome comic relief.

"Look, give it a few more days. A week at least. If nothing's happened by then I'll consider letting you go home."

He'd consider? Letting?

"I'll go home if I want, Blake, and there's nothing you can do to stop me."

Turning on her heel, she headed into the dining room. There weren't nearly as many people around the table as there would be later in the day. Most of the party crowd was probably still passed out from last night.

Peter sat beside her mother. As Anne and Blake walked into the room, he began gathering several papers and shuffled them back into a blank manila folder at his opposite elbow.

Anne sat two seats down from her mother, close enough that it didn't appear she was avoiding Marie, but with enough space that her neck didn't feel as if it would snap from the tension. Blake plopped down beside her.

"Good morning."

Marie glanced up, her mouth pinched into an unhappy line Anne didn't understand. She couldn't have done anything to deserve that look yet—she'd just gotten up for heaven's sake.

"Peter has informed the staff that you'll be dropping by the corporate offices today."

Anne flashed Peter an apologetic look. She was about to make his day difficult.

"I have no intention of going to the offices, Mother. I have a job. A job I'm good at. I will never work for Prescott Hotels."

"*Never* is a dangerous word."

Even now, knowing she had no tricks left up her sleeve, Marie was relying on her show of bravado and power to see her through. Anne had no compunction about disappointing her, even if she was dying.

"This company has been in the family for over one hundred years, young lady. You are the last remaining member of the Prescott line. The rightful head of the company."

That's not what her mother had said before Anne had walked out ten years ago. Then, she'd been told that there were plenty of other people who would jump through hoops to take her place. People who were more qualified. Now that the threat was hollow and the change in guard eminent, Marie's tune had definitely changed.

Anne supposed that, finally faced with her own mortality her mother had realized everyone else was either drug addled or without the sense God had given them.

"Then the vultures already circling will be ecstatic because I'll only be too happy to sell and give every damn cent to charity."

She shouldn't be so thrilled at the expression of outrage on her mother's face. However, she couldn't help feeling vindicated. In this, her mother had no control. But Anne could even take it one step further, push the knife in just a little more.

"Better yet. I'll set up a foundation in Michael's name. Definitely something to further gay rights. How much legislation do you think we could railroad through with the Prescott name and fortune?"

Her mother's face blanched. Marie's hands began to shake and for the first time Anne recognized she was goading a woman one step away from death. What was wrong with her?

Her mother tucked her hands beneath the table to hide the sign of weakness. Her color returned quickly, but not fast enough for Anne's conscience.

"All I'm suggesting, Annemarie, is that an intelligent businesswoman would at least want to take a look around and see what she was inheriting before giving it all away. Visit the office. Talk to the corporate team. View our quarterly statements. See what you're throwing away before you find out that the price of pride can be pretty damn high."

As if the woman knew anything about the price of pride. She would do whatever it took to keep up appearances, not caring about the ultimate cost. Michael was the purest example of that philosophy. If Marie had cared about her son half as much as she cared about her own image, Michael would still be alive.

Pushing away from the table, Marie stood up. Peter was immediately at her side, the folder tucked beneath his elbow and his hand grasped tightly around her arm. As they exited the room, Anne heard him ask if her mother felt up to working for a few hours.

Anne's chest tightened. She didn't want to feel anything for the cold woman who had raised her. Not compassion, not guilt, not fear on her behalf. As far as she was concerned, her mother was reaping what she'd sown. After being heartless and unfeeling for years, Marie was dying alone.

And yet Anne couldn't seem to stop herself from caring. She might not want to, but she did.

"I'll get a car. When do you want to leave?"

Blake's words had tears pushing to the corners of her eyes. How, after just weeks of knowing her, could he read her so well? How could he know without a doubt that guilt and remorse would drive her to do exactly as her mother had asked?

While her mother, a woman who shared half of her DNA, had never seemed to understand her at all?

"I HEARD HER TALKING about leaving, Peter. I can't have that. She's just finally come home."

He watched as she paced up and down in front of the fireplace in her office. Until recently it was a room she'd seldom used, preferring to spend her working hours at the corporate offices. But that had become more and more difficult with all the treatments, medications and their effects.

Despite the fact that her strides were hesitant and unsteady, she looked good today. At least better than he'd seen her in several days. Something told him the new surge of energy had been brought on by Annemarie's presence.

Marie Prescott now had a task to focus on. What she wanted—for her daughter to ascend the throne she'd built—was within her grasp. Or so she thought....

Little did Marie know that she wasn't the only one pulling puppet strings.

As he'd stared across the breakfast table at Annemarie, he'd been overwhelmed by conflicting urges—to reach across the table and slap her senseless for dismissing him out of hand and to wipe the anger and frustration away with the gentle touch of his fingers to her face.

"Peter! Are you listening to me?"

He clamped his muscles tight, refusing to jump at the sharp explosion of her voice into his thoughts. "Yes, ma'am. Sorry."

The word grated but he said it anyway. Continuing to bow down to her served his purposes at the moment, so he'd do it. That was one lesson Marie Prescott had never learned, humbling yourself on the outside meant nothing to the core of strength you held inside...especially if it lulled your enemy into a false sense of security.

"We need to find a way to convince her she's still in danger, because my illness doesn't appear to be enough to keep her here." Peter heard the bitterness in her voice and for the briefest moment was sad for her. He could understand the feeling of being disregarded by the one person you wanted attention from most. It had been a recurring theme throughout his entire life.

However, her concerns were valid. The last thing he wanted was for Annemarie to disappear again. It had taken months to discover her location the first time she ran away. This time, he didn't have months to wait.

She had to stay and finish this. She was the pawn he needed on the board to direct the other pieces in the game he was playing.

"Leave everything to me. I'll take care of it."

It was an office like many others she'd been in over the course of her corporate life. She'd felt right at home.

She hadn't wanted to.

It had been natural for her to walk into her mother's office, sit down behind her desk and start asking questions about the current expansion projects, newest locations and profit and loss statements for the almost three thousand worldwide properties.

The staff had treated her not only as if she belonged but as if she knew what she was doing. And she did. Her years of school and on-the-job training had prepared her...something she hadn't expected. She realized that today had been the softball stuff. It was easy to run a corporation this size when you employed good people and things were going well. The test always came when something went wrong.

A test she'd never find out if she was smart enough

and strong enough to pass because, after today, she wasn't coming back.

It would be too easy to step into Prescott Hotels. But she'd never wanted that. When she'd left she'd promised herself she'd be successful on her own terms, without the Prescott name or fortune. She couldn't do that if she took over as CEO of the whole damn thing.

She wanted something of her own. She wanted the life she'd built for herself.

She would not fall into the trap her mother had set.

Perhaps Marie knew her better than she thought—she'd chosen the perfect bait. Anne wouldn't put it past her to have told the staff to make Anne feel like a queen today just so she'd be tempted.

"You handled that all very well."

Blake had been her silent shadow throughout the day. They'd barely spoken. And yet at no time had she forgotten he was there, sitting quietly in a corner of her mother's office. Watching, always watching.

At one point she'd suggested he leave and come back for her later, promising that she wouldn't go anywhere without him. He'd just smiled and shaken his head. He'd even refused the newspaper she'd held out to him. Declining with a single word, he'd said, "Distraction."

"I seriously doubt someone will attack me in my mother's office," she'd argued. But that hadn't deterred him, either.

He'd watched her all day as she'd pored over reports, listened to junior executives and read financials. It had been unnerving, the way she couldn't shake the weight of his stare from her consciousness.

A less self-assured woman would have buckled under the power of his study. She'd simply started to burn, a slow, deep simmer that had the center of her panties wet with wanting him.

It was embarrassing that she had so little control over her own body.

"Stop looking at me like that." She deliberately kept her gaze down, refusing to meet his stare in an attempt to prevent the bubbling desire from boiling over. If she met his eyes, she wasn't sure exactly what she might do.

"Like what?" His rough voice melted into the tense silence that had surrounded them since the constant parade of people had ended. They'd been alone for a while now and she'd found it exceedingly difficult to concentrate on anything but him sitting there across the room. Waiting.

"Like you can't take your eyes off me. Like I'm the only thing on the planet that matters." Like he wanted to lick her up one side and down the other. Or maybe that was just her overactive imagination projecting. They'd been stuck inside the vast house together for three days and so far he hadn't so much as laid a finger on her.

She knew she should be happy about that, but her body told her she wasn't. She wanted his touch.

"I can't take my eyes off you," He said quietly. Unable to fight the urge any longer, Anne raised her gaze. "It's my job. I have to keep you safe."

His words said one thing, his eyes another. They were molten chocolate, churning and swirling with the same awareness she'd been fighting for hours. His body was tense, his fists wrapped tight around the arms of his chair as if that hold was the only thing keeping him from her.

Suddenly she wanted that hold to snap.

And in a blink of an eye, she got her wish. The

protesting creak of wood seemed to fill the room as he surged out of the chair and toward her. He was across the room in three strides, grasping her beneath the arms and lifting her out of her chair.

His hands braced her spine as he pressed her lower body into the desk and suspended her over the scatter of papers that had occupied her day. Before, they'd seemed so important; now she was ready to swipe them into a forgotten pile on the floor and use the desk for a better purpose.

His mouth descended on hers, forcing more from her than she'd intended to give. He opened her wide and plundered, his body arching over her, his hands holding her hard. He surrounded her and she felt her body melt in surrender as a sigh of relief slipped between them.

It had been four days since she'd felt the heat of him against her body. That was four days too long.

After several seconds of frantic male assertion, his hold on her eased. His hands became gentler, slipping across her body, searching for places that made them both shudder.

His palm found the smooth planes of her stomach, working its way up the inside of her blouse. She loved the feel of his callused hands against her smooth skin. He was skimming up the curve of her ribs to the swelling mounds of her breasts when a knock stopped them both cold. They froze, his fingers so close to where she wanted them that she could have wept in frustration.

Unfortunately, the rap on the office door had been more for show than courtesy.

"Ms. Prescott, I wanted to…"

Her mother's secretary trailed off into embarrassed silence, standing speechless in the open doorway, her face growing redder by the moment.

From her vantage point, Anne had to crane her neck back in order to see the other woman clearly. She could have done without the effort or the view. Turning away again, she quickly pulled herself together before pushing Blake away and straightening her clothes.

It should have been old hat, public displays of affection, her naked skin flashing for everyone to see. She hated the feeling of being watched. No, that wasn't quite right, she hated the idea of her and Blake being watched. What they shared was private. It didn't matter that there was one highly embarrassed woman standing there in awkward silence instead of a horde of camera-toting paparazzi. She still felt exposed and suddenly…dirty.

And that she didn't like. Nothing she and Blake had done deserved that kind of label.

Blake, smart man that he was, turned his back on them both, using the hulking desk chair to hide any telltale signs of arousal.

"Yes, Tina? What did you need?" Anne asked.

The other woman cleared her throat, shifting once from left to right before she regained her composure. Anne let her take whatever time she needed. Frankly, she needed those moments, too—her brain was still sluggishly clogged with desire.

"I, um, just wanted to ask if I could do anything for you before I left."

"No. No. You've been a great help. Thank you."

"My pleasure."

Tina glanced across Anne's shoulder at the man she knew stood silently behind her. In all honesty, Anne couldn't blame her for the stolen peek. She really wanted to look at him herself, to see if there were any overt signs of desire on his face and body as she feared there were on hers.

As Tina closed the door, Anne sank slowly into the chair behind her. Her gaze moved across the office, large, plush, perfect and somehow cold. Her mother's space. Prescott's corporate offices. What had she been thinking to let herself be carried away here of all places?

Ten years ago she might have laughed at the thought of disgracing her mother on her own turf. Now, the embarrassment was all hers. She wanted to drop her face into her hands and groan. Thank goodness she wouldn't actually be working here.

Blake slowly walked around the desk until he was standing across from her. She didn't know whether she should be grateful or disappointed that he'd put the piece of furniture between them. There was no question she thought what had just happened was a mistake, but some part of her didn't want him to feel that way.

She wanted him to be thoroughly disappointed that they'd been interrupted.

She looked up at him, her gaze traveling across his body. Unfortunately—or fortunately depending on how much she wanted to torture herself—the desk hid the most tempting piece of his anatomy. Anne let her eyes linger, enjoying the visual tour of his chest, arms, neck and face even if she couldn't actually reach out and touch.

There was no obvious sign of his desire—his muscles didn't appear to be tensed, and his jaw wasn't flexed with disappointment and barely leashed control—until she reached his eyes. Banked desire smoldered there if she wanted to fan those flames and continue what they'd started.

Oh, how she was drawn to that possibility.

But she kept her mouth shut and her hands folded quietly on the top of the desk.

Blake seemed to take that as a sign and asked, "Are you ready to go?"

With a nod, she gathered her stuff and headed out the door, determined to put what had just happened behind them.

Blake had gotten a car from George, preferring to drive them both himself, which was fine with her. They'd parked in a garage a couple blocks away. They could have had someone else bring them the car but Anne enjoyed walking through the brisk New York evening. Dusk was just falling and it helped to clear her head of the remnants of desire.

Once they reached the garage, Blake sped up to walk a couple paces ahead, reaching out to open the passenger-side door for her.

She barely had any warning, maybe the scuff of a rubber sole against the pavement but nothing to alert her to danger. Suddenly an arm wrapped around her shoulders, pinning both of her arms helplessly to her sides. A hand clamped down over her mouth, cutting off her scream of anger and terror before she could even utter it.

A wiry body full of sinewy strength crushed against her shoulder. He, she assumed it was a he, began dragging her backward between two cars. All she could think was to yell, to fight, to not go with whoever held her. She began kicking her feet, reaching out for anything she could damage. A grunt of pain whooshed past her ear when the heel of her pump grazed down the length of his calf. Good! But he didn't slow. Inch by inch, no matter how hard she jerked and fought, he pulled her away from the safety of the car. From the safety of Blake.

Surely Blake would notice what was going on, hear the struggle as they fought through a row of parked cars.

Although it felt like forever, it probably took all of thirty seconds before Blake appeared in her peripheral vision, brandishing a gun she hadn't even known he'd been carrying.

"Let her go."

The cold, hard menace in Blake's voice made her cringe even though she knew it was directed at her assailant and not her.

To her surprise, the man holding her not only stopped but in one giant heave, pushed her forward to the concrete floor. Her arms flailed, the sudden shift in her already off balance body too much to correct in time. One elbow, her chin and both knees struck the pavement with a sickening thud and a burst of pain.

She lay there for a moment, fighting to bring precious air back into her lungs. She'd had the wind knocked out of her once, falling from a swing set. She'd never been allowed on another again. It was the same sensation—as if she were drowning without a single drop of water— until her lungs finally reinflated.

Blake stopped at her side for one brief second before she heard his shoes bite into the floor as he gave chase. This was quickly followed by the loud squeal of tires pealing away. He wasn't gone long, barely enough time for her to catch her breath and roll over. The ceiling was in serious need of repainting.

What was wrong with her? She was rolling around in the grime of a parking garage floor. There was a madman on the loose, someone who'd just tried to abduct her, and all she could think of was that they needed a fresh coat of gray on a piece of concrete no one else had likely seen in twenty years.

A hysterical bubble threatened to escape her lungs. At least she had enough mental stability left to tamp it down.

She'd just struggled into a sitting position, propped against the tire of a dark-colored Buick when Blake appeared at her side. He crouched down, his eyes running the length of her body, probably cataloging how filthy she was. Despite everything, there was heat in his eyes. Heat and concern, and her traitorous body still reacted.

"Are you okay?"

Anne ran a mental checklist, moving various extremities as she did. "My knees hurt like hell and my jaw's a little sore, but I think I'm fine."

He reached down, pulled both her pant legs up past her knees and bent over her. The moist heat of his breath brushed across her suddenly exposed skin. The rush of cold January air followed along with a wave of goose bumps. He gently poked at her knees, picking up one leg and bending it this way and that.

Apparently satisfied with what he saw, he pulled her pants back down and grasped her chin gently between his fingers. He swiveled her face back and forth before returning her focus squarely to him.

His mouth was inches from her own. Despite the throbbing, protesting pain in her body, this seemed to be the only thing she could focus on. If she leaned just so, they'd meet. Her lips parted and her tongue darted out before she could stop the reaction to his nearness.

She watched his pupils dilate as he moved nearer, closing the gap by half.

It was a space of seconds, a breath of time, when she

thought for sure he would kiss her and make it all better. Instead, he pulled back and said, "You're a little banged up but you'll live."

The masochistic part of her was disappointed. The rest of her was just pissed. "What? Are you a doctor, too? Is there anything you can't do?"

"I can't seem to keep you safe."

Reaching down, he pulled her up off the pavement and into his arms. His hold was gentle though his tone had been anything but—cold and distant. She wound her arms around his neck and held on tight, wanting to envelop herself in his warmth and assure herself that she really was okay.

"But you did. You kept him from getting me."

When Blake looked down at her, she saw that his eyes matched the tone of his words. She really wanted the heat back instead of the remote, purposeful expression they now held. He weaved through the row of cars and settled her into the passenger seat.

Without another word he drove through the city, taking her home. Her knees ached and her jaw hurt like a son of a bitch and a big part of her wanted to return to that office, to the last five minutes they'd shared, and start over.

She wanted that Blake back.

10

"FIND OUT who's doing this, Blake."

That was precisely what he'd planned on, but it was nice to have Anne's endorsement. And her cooperation. At least she was willing to admit the danger was real now.

His hand smoothed the blanket over the side of the bed, running along the edge of her hip beneath the covers. They'd argued over whether she needed a doctor, but she'd pitched a big enough fit that he'd brought her directly back to the estate.

After a dose of extra strength painkillers and a washcloth to clean some of the street grime away from her skin, she was looking slightly better. Paler than he'd have liked, but feisty enough to fight with him. His mind told him her injuries were minor. The rest of him wanted to rip someone's head off for leaving the slightest mark on her skin.

But her abductor wasn't the only one responsible for the cuts and bruises on her body. He'd let himself get distracted…again. Why could he not keep his head in the game when she was around? He'd let that bastard

take her. No, she hadn't been seriously injured, but that
didn't help. She could have been.

He glanced at her face before quickly looking away.
The ugly bruise forming on her chin made his stomach
clench every time he saw it.

"Do you really mean that?"

"Of course!"

"Because that means me mucking around in your
life. Someone wants to hurt you and I need to figure
out why."

What puzzled him was the inconsistency of it all.
Break into her house but don't take anything. Take a
shot—a bad one—at her in a parking lot and then try
to abduct her. What was the purpose? To kill her? To
kidnap her? To get her out of the way?

The pieces just weren't fitting together.

"Nothing can be off-limits, Anne. In fact, I think you
need to start spilling your guts. Why would someone
want you dead or out of the way? What secrets do you
know?"

She laughed, a broken self-deprecating sound he really didn't like. "I don't know, for my money? For the
company? I have a lot of secrets, Blake. It'll take us days
to go through all of them. Most people have misspent
youths…. I misspent enough for an entire family."

"Why don't we start with why you left a cushy trust
fund and pampered existence behind to start a new life
in Alabama."

Her lips twisted into a grimace. "You've met my
mother."

"Yep. But that doesn't tell me what pushed you over
the edge *then*. Why that night? Why that week?"

She looked away from him, her lips thinning into a
line that told him he'd hit the soft spot on the first try.

Not that it had taken a genius. Most pampered heir-esses didn't leave the good life behind without a hefty shove.

He let her think. She either trusted him enough to do this or she didn't. Why was he strung so tight? Why was this moment, her decision, so important?

Without questioning what he was doing, Blake sank down onto the side of the bed and reached for her face. Gently, he forced her to look at him.

He didn't say a word, just stared steadily into her eyes and showed her that he was here, ready to listen. He'd trusted her from the moment they'd met, trusted her with the one secret he'd never told anyone else. Not that she realized it.

Maybe if he explained that to her she'd feel better about letting him into her life.

"You know that first night, the night I told you I got my tattoo in prison…? I wasn't kidding."

Her eyes widened into circles. "What? Karyn never told me."

"She wouldn't. She doesn't know. No one in the fam-ily does. I spent three months in jail for beating the shit out of the man who raped her. I didn't want the family to know. I didn't want Karyn to find out."

This time it was his turn to look away. It wasn't that he was ashamed of what he'd done—given the chance, he'd do it all over again. But he probably should at least feel some remorse.

He didn't.

"Why not?"

"She'd already had years of her life taken away wait-ing for justice to be served. When it wasn't, she found the will to move on with her life. I was so proud of her strength. I didn't want to bring the pain and memories back because I'd needed a chance for retribution. I was dishonorably discharged before my conviction was reversed on appeal. I didn't want her to feel guilty that I'd lost my job defending her. Besides, I'd never hear the end of it from Mama."

The ghost of a smile touched his lips because it was true.

He finally looked at her. "My point is, we all have secrets, Anne. I shared mine with you the first night we met. You can trust me with yours."

She stared at him for several seconds, weighing things out before she began talking. "I left one week to the day after I found my brother hanging from the ceiling of our hotel apartment in the city."

He was surprised to learn that her disappearance coincided with her brother's death although he probably shouldn't have been. He more than anyone understood how much her brother's pain and loss must have affected her.

As his perception shifted a little, the words continued to spill from her lips. "For months I'd called him a coward for keeping his sexuality a secret from Mother. He'd never even had to tell me, I'd just always known that's who he was. We both knew Mother wouldn't take it well, but I was tired of covering for him. I was tired of having to keep his secret. I wanted him to flaunt her rules, her ideas and her ways. I wanted him to hurt her the same way I did at every opportunity."

Blake watched as her eyes lost their shimmer. They dulled and turned inward, looking at the girl she used to be. He got the impression she wasn't happy with what she saw. Reaching out, he took her hand and offered silent support.

"I had no idea he'd planned on telling her that night.

Like always, I'd put on as little clothing as possible, grabbed a bunch of girls and gone to some club. I was looking to score—drugs, sex, I wasn't picky. About midnight I got a phone call from Michael. He was upset because he'd finally told Marie and things had not gone well. He asked me to come home, but I refused. It was early. I'd just started feeling fine and some random guy was sucking on my neck. My night was looking great. I told him I'd be there later and we could talk, that the worst was over and she'd get used to the idea. It was the last time I spoke to him. When I got home at four in the morning, he was dead."

Blake watched the silent track of a tear as it rolled down her face. He wasn't even sure she was aware that she was crying. Probably not, although from the sound of things she needed to. He wondered if she'd ever talked to anyone else about this.

"I stayed long enough to bury him and then I left and never looked back. I didn't even tell Marie where I was for months."

"You blame her." She'd told him as much on the plane and he could understand why she might. She needed to blame someone—both Marie and herself were easy targets for something that really only Michael could be held responsible for.

"Of course! If she'd been more tolerant. More understanding. Less…less *her* then it never would have happened."

She reached up and covered her face. "And if I'd been less me it never would have happened. If I'd been there, if he'd had someone to turn to…"

"You don't know that, Anne. Something else would have set him off. He would have waited until you weren't there. You can't live your life on maybes and what ifs. It happened and you learn to live with it and move on."

Right, like he was one to talk. Karyn had certainly found a way to move on with her life. And to anyone on the outside looking in, it probably appeared that he had his shit together, too. But they'd be wrong. He hadn't realized until Anne breezed into his life just how vacant it had become.

He rarely saw his family. He had employees but no real friends. For years the women in his life had been for sexual release and nothing more.

He was alone and had been for a very long time. Or he had been until Anne walked down that aisle and into his life.

"Which is exactly what I've been doing for the past ten years."

He wanted to argue with her on that point but didn't think now was the best time. She hadn't been living, either, and from what he could see she was far from moving on. She'd built a life, safe in the anonymity and undemanding requirements of it. No one judged her or watched her or asked her for anything.

But then no one really knew who she was. He knew this because he recognized the same safe cocoon he'd built around himself.

She could never truly be herself, she could never truly be open to the possibilities of a relationship while she was running away and hiding from the past. While she was letting guilt, fear and self-recrimination rule her decisions.

Just as he was.

But letting all of that go was easier said than done.

Did he want to live with the constant guilt? No, not anymore. Unfortunately, he had no idea how to shake it.

Perhaps they could find a way together. Of course, that assumed Anne would admit that she was lost in her past.

Until she did, there could be no future for them.

He hadn't realized just how tantalizing that prospect was until right now. He wanted a future. With her.

Just as soon as he was sure she'd be safe.

BLAKE REACHED for her, offering comfort she wouldn't allow herself to take. It would be so easy to cling to his strength. But she couldn't allow herself to depend on someone else who would disappear from her life eventually.

This was why she never talked about the past. This mind-numbing eternal loop of the mistakes she'd made and the heart-wrenching result. Most of the time she could forget, pretend that the girl she'd been was someone else. Not right now.

A shower. That's what she needed. Heat and steam and some way to relax and refocus. She needed something to do, something else to concentrate on.

Sliding off the opposite side of the bed, Anne looked down at Blake. His hip was propped on the edge, right where her body had been. She wanted desperately to lie back down, to pull him there with her. Which was why she turned around and kept going. "I'm taking a shower," she said, looking briefly over her shoulder. The words were emotion clogged and almost desperate, but that didn't matter.

The minute the bathroom door closed and locked behind her, Anne stripped her clothes off. She was naked as she flipped on each and every light, flooding the large space with a cheery brightness.

The water was like ice when she first turned it on. She stepped into the stream anyway; it was still warmer than her skin. Suddenly her teeth were chattering. Guilt or delayed shock from earlier?

She stood as the pelting spray warmed. It thawed her by degrees, the blazing heat barely registering as her mind continued to fly around and around. Maybe the bathroom hadn't been the best choice. While it wasn't the same room she'd found her brother in, the memories were too close to the surface right now.

The walls, a sand-colored marble began to waver around her. No. That wasn't right. They couldn't move. Maybe she was the one moving. She wasn't still trembling though—her teeth had finally clenched together. Her lungs heaved, gulping in the steam-laden air as quickly as they could.

That's when the tears started.

And they wouldn't stop. She backed away from the pounding water until her back slammed into the cold stone of the shower wall. Her battered knees gave out and she slid down the wall onto the floor with a wet plop. A rain of bottles, a razor and a metal can of shaving cream all hit the floor around her in a loud clatter.

She'd never cried for him. She'd never let the river of emotions go because she'd been afraid once that dam had burst, she wouldn't be able to pull them all back. Her mother's cold stare had kept Anne's emotions at bay during the funeral. Prescotts did not show the world their pain.

From there she'd been too busy escaping, hiding, surviving, to let herself grieve. After a while it had seemed pointless. Crying would not bring Michael back. It would not change the role she'd played in his death.

Some part of her even thought it would lessen the sharpness of the guilt she felt. That was something she hadn't wanted. She wanted the constant reminder of the girl she'd been. She needed that barrier against the life she'd once led.

Anne's tears poured out in huge, racking sobs, taking with them years of bottled-up grief.

Now she was well and truly alone, without even the sharpness of Michael's memory beside her.

BLAKE HAD SETTLED gingerly into a chair in the corner of the room, the back of it leaning against the shared wall with the bathroom. He'd wait for her, for however long she needed to be alone.

Until he heard a crash that sounded as if everything in the entire bathroom had just hit the floor.

Jerking up from the chair, he knocked on the door. "Anne? Are you all right?"

There was no response.

He tried again, a little louder. Nothing.

He grasped the knob and turned it, only to find it was locked. And all he could see in his mind was her, despair filling her eyes, tears tracking down her face, and suddenly knew he had to get to her. Now.

Rearing back, he aimed his foot right beside the lock on the door and kicked. It took several tries, but with each time the wood buckled until it finally gave with a resounding crack.

The sound of running water was loud in his ears. He didn't like the edge of panic he was fighting down. It left him feeling vulnerable and out of control. A sensation he hadn't experienced since the night his mother had called to tell him what had happened to Karyn.

A haze of steam drifted around him, creating an eerie, out-of-body feeling. His eyes found her through the clouds that filled the room, swirling thicker around her body, entrapped by the marble and glass walls. She was gorgeous, every bit as flawless as his memory insisted.

Her skin glowed pale pink in the heat. Droplets of water rolled slowly down the curve of her spine to collect at the swell of her ass. The water rolled off, like a waterfall.

Her hair, darker now, clung to her back in a sheet of silk. She shook her head back and forth, feathering the edges against her skin in a way that made his insides clench down hard on the desire to do the same with his hands...his lips.

And then he realized she was propped against the side of the wall, her body hunched in over itself.

He must have made a sound, because suddenly her head snapped around and the breath blew out of his body with a whoosh. Her eyes dug into him, devastated, as they connected through the glass.

Oh hell.

Without saying a word, he pushed against the door and opened it. She reached for him, wrapping a warm, wet hand into the center of his shirt. When had he moved close enough for her to reach him?

Anne yanked, using the leverage of surprise to move him forward. He would have tripped on the lip of the shower and fallen at her feet if his hands hadn't caught the cold marble.

"What are you doing?"

"I want you."

Her voice was soft and rough, her throat protesting even those small words.

"I'm fully clothed."

"I don't care."

His eyes narrowed on her face and he wasn't happy with what he saw. At first the water beating down on her skin disguised her swollen eyes and puffy face. The thought of her in here alone, wrecked and crying made him cringe.

She needed him right now. And he was bastard enough to take advantage of that for the both of them. To hell with the consequences, they'd deal with them later.

She slammed the glass door shut behind him, wrapping them both in the thick steam and the overwhelming scent of her. He was soaked within seconds, unable to avoid the stinging spray. It scalded. How could she stand it? But when his hands finally touched her skin he understood. She was smooth and perfect and barely warmed through.

Reaching behind her, he turned the temperature down.

"What are you doing?"

"I prefer not to boil."

"Stop. I'm cold."

Delayed shock. Why hadn't he thought of that in the first place? Of course she was cold…and scared. Any normal human would be after what she'd gone through today.

He'd take this slow, warm her up and give her what she needed—a reminder that she was fine and alive.

Water saturated his clothes, pressing down against

his body and—combined with the thick wall of steam shrouding them both—increased the sensation of being crowded, smothered by his own desires.

Anne pressed her body to him and through the conductor of drenched denim and cotton, he could feel every curve, dip and sigh. Her eyes closed as her head dropped back into the stream of water. Bliss. That was the only word to describe the expression on her face, and it had his insides spasming in pain. He was about to lose it and that was the last thing she needed.

He closed his eyes.

Bad idea.

The second they shut his other senses went on red alert. The scent of her overwhelmed him, filling his body, saturating his lungs. The sound of her breathing, as labored and tortured as his own, seemed to scream in his ears.

He swore he could feel her heartbeat, faster than it should be, thumping from her chest into his own. The soul-deep sensation of the rhythmic flutter was unexpected and arousing. Every square inch of his body began to throb and tingle where it touched hers.

His hands clenched the wet strands of her hair, needing something solid to keep him grounded in reality. This. The two of them. Wasn't real.

He unfurled each of his fingers, one at a time, trying to pull back and give himself some space to find his control. His arms dropped to his sides. His wet clothes stayed behind for a fraction of a second, suctioned to her body as if they were reluctant to let her go.

Her eyes popped open then, a shiver snaking down her spine. She looked at him. Really looked. Her eyes holding him still in midretreat. He watched the green irises, clearer now than they'd been minutes before, darken and glitter. His breath caught in the back of his throat increasing the already suffocating sensation of being drowned by a cloud of steam.

"No."

11

"Don't go."

She didn't want him to leave. And she was willing to do whatever it took to keep him right here with her.

Placing a hand in the center of his chest, she stepped forward. She didn't stop when her body came flush with his, although the temptation was there. Instead she kept pushing, urging him backward into the cooler part of the shower. Air hissed through his clenched teeth as his back hit the cold marble.

Anne reached for the hem of his shirt, pulling the soaked cotton up his body and over his head in one smooth motion. It made a wet squelching sound as it smacked into the opposite corner and fell to the floor. Her hands touched him then, curling into his chest. She needed to touch more of him, to touch something inside of him just as he'd coaxed her to show him the deepest parts of herself.

Her palms ran down his chest, wiping away droplets of water that clung to the dark hair there. It was rough against her hands, his skin slick and giving beneath her explorations.

Beads of moisture clung to her own skin and she

felt a thrill of power when his eyes hooked onto one. Mesmerized, he watched it roll past the jut of her collarbone. Gravity grabbed hold and pulled it down, slipping along her skin from shoulder to breast. It held there for a moment, perched at the edge of her swollen nipple. She probably wouldn't have felt its gentle slide across her skin if not for the extra weight his stare gave the bead of water. She wanted him to reach for it with his tongue, but he didn't lean forward before it fell to join the growing pool at their feet.

She leaned into his body, her mouth meeting his. She knew the moment he was lost to the same sucking force that swirled inside her body. She watched his eyes glaze with desire.

He plundered, taking everything she offered and more. What she'd started as a cool, calm kiss he turned into an inferno of desire—desire he'd been holding back for too many days.

His hands captured her hair, cradling the curve of her head and the graceful column of her neck. He manipulated her, holding her tighter to his body, not allowing her any quarter against the drive building inside them both.

She wanted this. She wanted him.

Sounds leaked from her throat, guttural urgings for harder, faster, more. Her fingers curled into the waistband of his sodden jeans, tugging the fabric away without taking the time to undo the fly. With frantic fingers, he reached down and freed the button and zipper for her. The material wouldn't cooperate. It clung to him, scraping and sucking at his skin.

Finally, his pants hit the wall, too. She let out a sigh of relief, knowing nothing was going to stop them this time.

He reached for her, lifting her up and plastering her body against his.

She closed her eyes, raising her face to the steam in thanksgiving. The feeling was sensational, better than anything she'd ever known.

He walked back through the spray of water, shielding her face from the pounding stream with his own body. It was her turn to suck in a shocked breath as her back connected with the chilled stone of the wall. The contrast made her writhe against the warm hardness of Blake and the cold unyielding weight at her back.

Her hands grabbed the back of his hair, tugging until his head dropped forward. Her mouth found the hollow of his throat. His contented purr tickled against her skin as she ran teeth and tongue across his throat.

Anne hitched one leg high on his hip, opening the core of her body to him. She was as wet and hot as the steaming water around them. She wanted him inside, quenching the ache that was building to unbearable.

Her body shifted, searching for the one thing that could turn that ache to liquid fire. A groan of satisfaction slipped out of her when she finally aligned their bodies, her swollen sex against his.

But he didn't plunge in. And she was powerless to make him, drowning in a sensual pool she had no willpower to escape.

Instead, he rocked his hips against her, increasing the friction between them. Leaning down to her shoulder, he lapped at a trail of water droplets on her skin, following it to the swell of her breast.

He circled her swollen flesh with his tongue, making sure he collected each and every drop. She whimpered as he studiously ignored the pinched and aching point waiting for him in the center.

Finally, he flicked his tongue out, taking the tiniest taste of her. Her knees buckled, her body sagging harder against him. His arms tightened around her, making sure she couldn't fall to the floor and hurt herself.

He reached for her other leg, wrapped it tight around his waist and pulled her harder against his body. His arms balanced, one beneath her and the other around her, using the wall at her back to brace them both.

Her body was slick from the water, his own skin pressing and sucking where they joined. Friction continued to build between them as she moved against him, reaching up with her mouth to claim his lips again. Her legs were tight bands around him, squeezing and flexing, urging him on to what they both wanted.

Her sex brushed against his throbbing cock. She used her own strength to clench and release the muscles in her thighs, rocking her body up and down him. She enjoyed watching his eyes glaze at the pleasure she could give him. At any moment either of them could have reached down and put them both out of their misery. But they didn't, each wanting to prolong these precious stolen moments.

Blake's breath panted through his lungs in short, hot bursts that told her he was nearing the end of his control. That knowledge only increased the heat coursing through her own blood. Soon. Soon, they'd both be on fire.

Or that's what she thought until Blake laid his forehead against her, his eyes closed, his face strained. "Please tell me there's a condom somewhere close by?"

His question stilled her for a moment. She appreciated the gesture he'd just made. Anne had been so far gone she never would have stopped to wonder about protection. She wrapped her hands around his jaw, lifted his face so he would look at her and smiled. "Bedside table."

"Thank God."

On a sigh of relief, Blake tightened his arms more firmly around her body, reached blindly behind to shut off the water and walked them both from the shower into the bedroom.

Cool air rushed across her damp skin, her body tightening against the chill in a way that only increased her pleasure. Blake dropped her gently to the bed, and Anne lounged back on half-bent elbows. She looked up at Blake, watched him.

He was big and broad, altogether male. His body was hard where it should be, toughened by years of discipline and training. She'd loved how they fit together during the one night they'd shared and shivered at the thought of finally experiencing that again.

Her legs sprawled out between them. One knee was bent and slightly raised from the bed, as if to give him a place to start. The other was curved and comfortable, leaving her body open to his gaze.

He reached for her, running his hand slowly from the curve of her calf to her inner thigh. Her breath caught in her lungs when he reached higher, his fingertips skimming the outside folds of her sex. Her body tensed, asking for more.

His knees hit the bed. She moved, opening the space at the center of her body, making room for him. He placed his cheek to the bent curve of her knee, running the stubble-roughened skin back and forth against her inner thigh as his eyes bored into her soul.

His mouth followed the trail his fingers had taken, kissing and licking his way to the center of her body.

His lips grazed the nest of curls there, doing no more than tempting them both.

His tongue dipped into her heat, laving across the opening to her body. She gasped, a hard sound of pleasure, and lifted her hips for more. He gave it to them both, licking harder, deeper, higher, making her lose herself in the sensation of him.

They were both panting when he stopped. Her body was bowed tight, the muscles bunching hard on the prelude to a climax he'd denied her.

Blake reached across to the bedside table, yanked it open and pulled out a handful of foil wrappers. Condoms spread across the bed like a trail of crumbs leading home. He tore at one, quickly rolling it down the length of his erection.

Anne threw her head back, her eyes no more than slits as she watched him protect them both. He wrapped his arms around her, pulling her close even as his lips found hers again.

He slid his tongue into her mouth at the same time his cock slipped inside her body. She gave easily, wrapping her legs tight around his waist and locking him to her. She arched into him as he slowly pumped in and out. The sensation was electric, even better than the first time, which was saying a whole hell of a lot. Of course, neither of them had overindulged in alcohol this time. They were both sanely sober.

Her fingernails scraped down his spine. The muscles of his back were taut beneath her hands. He continued to stroke in and out of her body, release waiting for them both, a dark beckoning devil of bliss.

She was so close. And she wanted that feeling of ecstasy now.

"Come for me." The words were a whispered command against her skin. If she'd been able to think, she would have ignored such a command on sheer principle.

But her body responded, tightening around him, weeping and spasming her release. Her mouth opened on a silent cry but her eyes stayed locked with his.

Her one victory was that her orgasm vaulted Blake into his own, brought there by the urging of her body. His control lasted no longer than her own.

With a groan of utter abandon, Blake collapsed onto the bed beside her, physically spent. His body sprawled across her, one arm thrown over her chest and a leg wrapped high over her hip. She didn't mind. In fact, she enjoyed the weight of him against her body, something she'd never liked before.

In the past, the moment she'd come she'd always wanted away from the man who'd given her the release. But this was different. Blake was different. She suddenly had the urge to snuggle against him, bury her nose in his skin and suck his scent into her lungs.

So she did. Her lips curled. She figured he could probably feel the curve of her satisfied smile against his skin. So what? A sound rolled through her body. Surprisingly, it resembled a sound Prada made, a growling, purring satisfaction.

"Thank you."

She had no idea how long they lay there. Maybe minutes. Maybe an hour. It didn't matter. But she could pinpoint the exact moment when reality started horning in on their afterglow. She could almost hear the wheels turning in his mind and could feel the tension as it seeped into his body.

She waited, but it didn't take long. His words turned

her pliant muscles hard. "So, are you going to disappear again?"

Damn it. She shouldn't have been surprised and probably deserved the question, all things considered. But that didn't mean she wanted to deal with it now.

With a little huff of displeasure so he'd know where they stood, she rolled to lie flat on the bed. She still touched him, because she couldn't make herself move away from him completely, but no longer curled into his body like she really wanted to.

"Where would I go?"

Blake turned his head and propped himself up on one elbow so that he could look down at her.

"I think you know what I mean. I don't just mean physically, although you certainly do that well. I mean, are you through pretending this—" he waved his hand back and forth between them "—isn't happening?"

She turned to stare straight into his direct gaze. "I don't know. Are you?"

He frowned. What she really wanted was to reach up and run the pad of her thumb across his lips. Instead she said, "We've both done plenty of running, although I admit I started it. But, yeah, there's no reason to deny ourselves this. At least until you go home."

She'd expected his frown to ease; instead the crease in between his eyebrows got deeper. "Here. Only here. I won't take the chance of being distracted when we're out in public. Not again."

She shrugged. Just as well.

He was sprawled across her bed, wet, rumpled and sexy as hell. Her personal plaything. Something about that was less than satisfying. She wanted more from him than sex, although that was all she really had reason to hope for.

Suddenly she felt the urge to flee. To get away from him before he broke her heart like every other person in her life who'd ever mattered.

But she wanted him. Despite knowing in her heart he'd hurt her—he might not mean to but the result would be the same when he walked away. Perhaps that was why she'd run out on him a month ago. Even then she'd known this would happen if she let it.

She cared for him. Part of her hated herself for that. For the weakness of it.

He reached for her, tucking her body into the curve of his own and pulling a blanket over them both. His warmth and scent wrapped around her, more comforting than the blanket ever could be.

A lethargic peace stole over her. The events of the past few hours finally slammed into her, dragging her closer and closer to oblivion.

Just before she gave in to the urge to let go, she felt his fingers brush softly against her face. His lips touched the crown of her head as he whispered into her hair, "Sleep."

She'd never felt safer in her life.

BLAKE WATCHED Anne sleep. He knew she hated it when people watched her, but he couldn't help himself and she was dead to the world and would never know it. He imagined she hadn't gotten much rest lately and liked the idea that she felt comfortable enough with him to let herself go.

But he couldn't settle. The conversation they'd had played over and over again in his mind, keeping him from completely relaxing beside her.

She wouldn't run away again. She'd given him her word, although her response had been less than euphoric.

He supposed it was the best he was going to get at the moment. The fact that she'd given in at all should shock him. He should be happy he'd gotten that much out of her.

So why did he feel as if he'd won the lottery only to realize he'd washed the ticket with his pants? He'd won...at least on this one point. But it was a hollow victory.

When all this was over, she'd simply cut him out of her life. The problem was, the longer he was around her the more time he wanted to spend with her. She was easily becoming just as addictive as any drug he'd ever heard of.

Worse, because when she was gone there'd be no way for him to get another fix.

Her throwing him aside wasn't the only thing he had to worry about. Everything had happened so quickly tonight, he hadn't had the chance to dwell on the latest threat.

Someone had tried to kidnap Anne.

And the man had almost succeeded. If Blake had been a few seconds slower with his reaction time, she would have been gone, headed for God only knows what kind of torture.

That thought made him even more restless. The sheet was suddenly too heavy against his clammy body. Throwing the covers back, he was careful not to wake her as he slipped from the bed.

He'd been distracted again. His head—and his throbbing erection—had still been back at Marie's office. If his head had really been in the game he'd have noticed the man lurking in the shadows. Wouldn't he?

He hoped so, because the thought that he might not

be able to protect her sent a cold shiver of dread racing through his body.

He'd vowed to keep his hands off her. That vow hadn't lasted very long.

But maybe this was for the best. She'd agreed they'd be together only here in the house. He was relatively comfortable with her safety here. Besides—he looked at the gun on the dresser—his weapon wouldn't be far away. This way he could take off the edge at night, hopefully leaving his head clear of the desperation to touch her during the day.

This was better than his vow to keep his hands off her. It had to be.

Which reminded him, he needed to let Marie know what had happened this evening. As much as keeping her in the loop grated on him, she was Anne's mother and had a right to know. He knew his mama would freak if she found out someone had tried to kidnap Karyn and no one had bothered to tell her. He could only imagine Marie's frigid response to the lapse in security protocol.

Looking around, he quickly realized a problem. What he'd worn in here was still in a sopping heap on the shower floor. Picking up the phone, he called the housekeeper and requested two robes be brought to Anne's room. He wasn't sure if she had one or not but figured while he was asking…

He stood at the door, waiting for the sound of footsteps so he could intercept the housekeeper before she knocked and woke Anne. Sticking his head out of a crack in the doorway, he grasped the bundle of soft velour she held out and thanked her.

Once he was decent he headed across the hallway to his own suite to don more appropriate clothing. No sense in flashing their change in status to Marie. He got the impression she wouldn't be happy about that at all. He knew she didn't like him. Not that he cared.

They had one common goal and that was keeping Anne safe.

It didn't take him long to find the older woman, settled into a warm sitting room by herself. A fire crackled in the grate of a fireplace large enough to roast an entire pig. The light was low, the surroundings rather sad in their austerity. Loneliness seemed to permeate the entire space.

He watched Marie straighten her shoulders when he entered the room, putting on the Prescott mantle she wore so well. He wondered if the weight of it ever got to her. Probably not. She seemed to enjoy everything that came with the position as head of the family and company.

"What do you want, Mr. Mitchell?"

Her frigid tone made him wonder if she already knew what he and her daughter had been up to. It was entirely possible that she had the whole house under constant surveillance. He could just imagine a group of security personnel sitting in front of a bank of monitors, watching all the hallways and doorways.

"Did you know that someone took a shot at Anne back in Birmingham? Broke her windshield. Or that Anne was almost kidnapped tonight."

"What?" The surprise on her face was unmistakable. He had briefly wondered if Marie had been behind everything that had happened to Anne. Her daughter certainly believed the woman was capable of just about anything in the name of getting what she wanted. He'd become increasingly suspicious of Marie since nothing more had happened once they'd gotten here.

Not until this evening, at least.

"How could this happen? I thought you were protecting her!"

The barb hit a bit too close to home, which made his response a little harsher than normal. "She's safe, isn't she? He didn't get her."

"Tell me exactly what happened."

Blake provided the details, as many as he had. He described the man when she asked, as much as the assailant's black mask and nondescript clothing would allow. He did mention one small detail that he'd forgotten about until his brain began running over the scene again in slow motion.

While the clothing and shoes the man wore had spoken of discount store prices, half of the dial of an expensive watch had poked free from the dark sleeve of his shirt.

His words trailed off as he described that last piece of information. Marie collapsed back into her chair, an unexpected expression of relief stamped onto her drawn features.

She was silent for several moments. When she finally looked up at him again, the hard edge he'd come to expect from her shrewd blue eyes was back.

"Thank you for protecting my daughter, Mr. Mitchell. I will of course provide you with a bonus for your service."

Her words pissed him off. He had no intention of taking her money, especially for something he damn well would have done for Anne no matter what her circumstances.

"Don't bother."

PETER WATCHED as Mitchell slipped back into Annemarie's room. His jaw tightened with anger and disbelief.

The slut had let him into her bed.

Didn't she realize she was his? Had always been his. Would always be his.

He'd forgiven her the transgressions of her youth. Everyone needed to sow some wild oats and he'd understood her desire to experience every kind of pleasure opened to her. After all, he'd felt the same way and had no problems with exploring the more aggressive possibilities of sex. He'd experimented with men, women, both together. Pain, submission, domination. They all had their pleasures, although in some small corner of his mind he'd always reserved a pristine corner for what he and Annemarie would experience.

He'd always known her affairs were meaningless. And he hadn't been ready for her. They hadn't been ready for each other. Underneath it all he'd always known they would fit together perfectly, not only complimenting each other in the physical sense but in an emotional one, as well.

She'd been the brightness he'd always needed in his life. The laughing, garish, beautiful light.

But Mitchell was different. Peter had never known Annemarie to take the same man into her bed twice. He wasn't about to let their little dalliance derail all his plans and hard work. Annemarie was destined for greatness. Was destined for him.

Together they could rule it all. With her by his side he'd have access to the Prescott fortune, the Prescott name, the Prescott corporation and the added benefit of Annemarie's body waiting in his bed.

He needed her. He wanted her. He'd have to teach her a lesson, to remind her where her place would always be. He hated to hurt her, but it was for her own good. The sooner she realized the rules of her new life, the sooner she'd learn to find happiness in what he had planned for them both.

He had no doubt she would come to heel. Because pain was a stronger motivator than fear.

12

HER STOMACH RUMBLED and woke her. The churning sensation wasn't very pleasant, but the voice beside her was.

"Welcome back to the living."

Anne could feel him, wrapped around her body, one arm thrown over her waist, one leg wedged between her own. It took several moments for her brain to start firing on all cylinders, for her to register the way her own arm was possessively draped over the curve of his shoulder, fingers entwined in his hair.

His eyes smiled down at her and she realized how tightly she actually clung to him—as if he'd tried to get away from her while she slept and she'd clamped on, unwilling to let him go.

"How long have I been asleep?" How long had she held him prisoner?

Blake rolled the arm at her back and peeked over her shoulder, she assumed, at the watch on his wrist.

"About six hours. It's a little after one."

"In the morning?" She realized it was a stupid question considering the only light in the room came from the milky moonlight at her back.

She wasn't sure what she wanted more, to snuggle deep under the covers and take advantage of the fact that Blake was still beside her or to eat. Her stomach rumbled again, loudly, making the decision for her.

Blake laughed. "Let's feed you."

Bounding from the bed, she glanced around the room for the clothes she'd been wearing, and realized they were still in a heap on the bathroom floor. Blake's arms wrapped around her, a fluffy velour bathrobe in one hand.

"Try this." His lips touched the outer shell of her ear. His teeth took a teasing nip at her before easily letting her go. He put on a bathrobe, as well.

She had no idea where the robes had come from, but didn't care. Hers was a pale pearl-gray, his a deep burgundy. The open folds settled over his chest, revealing a wide swath of skin and light dusting of hair. For a moment Anne could do nothing but stare at him.

Her brain shortcircuited for a second.

"What's wrong?"

"Nothing." She shook her head, hoping to force her mind to start functioning again. When he was around, nothing else mattered.

And that was a problem of huge proportions.

She didn't like the way he took over her senses and called to the most primitive parts of her being. When she let that side of her reign, bad things happened.

He was bad for her. Anything this good, anything this pleasurable, had to be. She'd learned that the hard way.

"Not nothing." He reached for her, running a finger down the center of her forehead and over the bridge of her nose. "You're frowning. What's wrong?"

She couldn't tell him the truth—doing that would

give him more power over her than he already had. Instead she clung to the one thought that might satisfy him.

"I'd prefer no one see us. I was just wondering if anyone else was around."

His response was immediate. The lingering warmth and satisfaction disappeared from his deep, dark eyes. His jaw pulled tight as he turned away.

"Don't worry. I doubt anyone's up at this hour." His voice was clipped and that alone made her regret her words.

But it was too late to take them back. She wrapped the bathrobe around her and led the way as they slipped through the dark and quiet house. They had the kitchen to themselves, the staff having retired hours ago. Her mother would have a conniption if she found out her daughter had even set foot in the room.

They had people for that.

It didn't take Anne long to pull out the makings for sandwiches. Cold cuts, cheese, bread, mayo, lettuce, tomato. She piled one high for Blake. After watching him eat over the past several days, she knew the man had an appetite.

Thinking about Blake's appetite had her own stirring to life. Not her hunger for food but her hunger for him. Ignoring the pangs, she passed him a plate and reached behind her for a soda from the refrigerator. Tossing him the can, she leaned against the counter and dug into her sandwich.

He bit into his, chewing slowly and staring at her, his head cocked slightly to the side.

"What?"

He swallowed, took another bite and swallowed again before answering her. "Nothing. Just not exactly how

I'd expected today to end, eating sandwiches standing at the kitchen counter with you."

A laugh burst from her. "No, not your typical Prescott affair. There's no silver or platinum-edged goblets." Holding up a potato chip, she continued, "Certainly not haute cuisine."

He smiled, as well, finally releasing the tension he'd been carrying. For the first time since they'd walked out of her room she felt as if she could breathe.

"You really don't fit here, you know."

"Where? In the kitchen?" The comment shouldn't have hurt, but somehow, coming from him it did. That he couldn't see her as normal bothered her. She'd thought he had seen beneath the Prescott facade...beneath even the mask she'd worn for a decade.

But maybe she should be glad he hadn't.

"No. You definitely belong here. It's the rest of the place that doesn't suit you."

Somehow that wasn't much better. She didn't belong in her old life. She didn't belong in her new one, either. She didn't belong anywhere.... Although her body told her the one place she did belong was in Blake's bed.

"Don't get me wrong, I can imagine you here, years ago, the party girl, but now... I know you could handle anything from state diners to down and dirty rocker parties, but I can't see you being comfortable here. Day after day after day."

He set his plate on the counter, his meal completely forgotten.

"A week ago, after seeing your designer shoe collection and that trendy cat, I would have said this was exactly where you belonged."

He took her plate away, as well, leaving her hands empty. She curled them into balls to keep herself from reaching for him. Why? Because in that precise moment she'd never wanted anything more in her entire life than to touch him. And the force of that need scared the hell out of her.

She didn't know him. She didn't want him. She didn't need him. She didn't.

Maybe if she said it long enough she'd start believing it.

She needn't have bothered with the effort because he clearly wasn't concerned that she hadn't touched him. He took care of that for the both of them.

His hands framed the sides of her face, his palms warm against her skin. His fingers slid into her hair, gently massaging her scalp. Waves of awareness rippled from her head to her toes, lapping at her senses and eroding her sanity as surely as any outgoing tide.

And then his mouth claimed hers. He wasn't gentle. He wasn't kind. But he was insistent and thorough and unbelievably arousing. His tongue slid easily into her waiting mouth. There wasn't any effort here, just the muffled sigh of her surrender and his light groan of desire. It was easy. And perfect.

He meant to pull back. Anne could feel the intention as his muscles coiled, but that wasn't what she wanted. She wanted this moment to go on forever, for it to blot out everything but the storm of emotions he could pull from the center of her soul without even trying.

For the first time in ten years Anne felt both completely in control and utterly uninhibited. A delicious combination of the two lives she'd created—the past and her present. Never, in her entire life, had she experienced the best of both those worlds at the same moment.

She'd always thought that they precluded each other— the ruthless control beating out the wicked impulses. But she'd been wrong. In Blake's arms she could have them both. And she was greedy enough to take that sensation whenever she could get it. Because she knew it wouldn't last.

Anne reached for him, wrapping her fingers in the collar of his robe and pulling him tight against her body. "No. Don't go."

His heavy eyes gazed at her, and she could see him make the decision. She loved to watch his brain work, the quick and thorough way he analyzed every angle of every situation and came to the exact right conclusion at the perfect time.

She envied him that speed and confidence. Despite the outer shell she showed the world, she didn't think she was ever as sure of herself as Blake appeared to be.

"You're always so sure, aren't you?"

His hands wrapped around her hips, lifting her onto the island counter that had been pressing gently into her back.

"What do you mean?"

He didn't pause for her answer. Instead, he opened the V of her robe wider and latched his lips to the curve of her throat. She tipped her head back to give him better access, wanting the feel of him there even more than he wanted to touch her.

"I mean, you never waiver, never stop. You make a decision and you go with it. Don't you ever wonder if you've made a mistake?"

"Where is this coming from?"

His hands touched the inner curve of her thighs, naked beneath the thick gray cloth around her. She opened for him in an instant. The feel of his hands brushing up the length of her skin had heat pouring into her veins. It pooled at the center of her sex, a wet warmth gathering there.

She shook her head, no longer caring about the conversation. She just wanted him to touch her. Anne shifted her hips, trying to bring his fingers in contact with her aching body.

His hands stilled on her thighs. "I don't have the luxury of making mistakes. I make a mistake and someone gets hurt. You get hurt." The corners of his eyes pinched at the intrusion she'd inadvertently brought between them.

The heat of his hands on her body now contrasted to the cold coming off him in waves. Wanting to pull him back into the moment with her, she reached for him. A quick tug and she released the belt on his robe, the sides falling open with the quiet slide of fabric against skin.

That snapped his attention back to where she wanted it. His eyes quickly heated through once more and a satisfied smile tugged at the corners of his lips.

He was glorious. And for the moment he was hers.

She touched his chest, laying her palms flat and letting them play across the hard muscles there. Her eyes followed her motions, drinking in the perfection of his body. He might not be a soldier anymore but he'd certainly maintained the physique.

His erection stood out from his torso, long, hard and insistently flawless. Her hands curled around his waist, digging in and pulling him the last few inches toward her.

Blake reached for the tie to her robe, tugging it slowly open. His chocolate eyes blazed at her, deep and intense. There was no smile now, no conversation, no thoughts other than the urge to touch and take.

His hands were rough against her skin as he raced

them once down the length of her body. She didn't mind. She enjoyed the reminder that she was soft and feminine, delicate.

His fingers dipped into the folds of her sex, spreading the slick moisture of her arousal as he went. Her eyes lowered to watch him play.

He slipped a single finger inside. That wasn't what she wanted. Wasn't him. But it felt so good she couldn't find the words to tell him to stop. He worked her, kneading and touching the pleasure point deep inside, brushing his thumb back and forth across her clit in an increasing rhythm that matched her quickening breath.

She was so close. She could feel it, the tightening deep inside right before the explosion. And just as she was about to find the strength to tell him to stop—because she wanted *him*—something else did it for her.

A loud crash sounded from somewhere in the house, like glass and wood shattering.

"What the—"

Blake, as always, was quicker to respond than she. In seconds flat he'd removed his hands from her body, grasped her waist and pushed her behind his tall frame. He took a quick glance around as he retied the sash at his waist before turning to do the same for her. She batted him away.

"Stay here," he growled, snagging a butcher knife from the block on the counter as he left the kitchen. She ignored him, following quickly into the formal rooms of the house.

She wasn't sure what she'd expected to find. Her strung-out aunt unconscious in a pile of glass possibly. Or one of her cousins passed out drunk across a broken piece of furniture. The knife grasped in his tight fist said Blake expected trouble in some form.

What she wasn't anticipating was the vision of her mother, blood dripping down her forehead and arm, unconscious on the floor of the living room. She looked dead, her broken body on top of a pile of wood and glass that used to be a bookshelf.

Anne wasn't prepared for her feelings of emptiness and despair at the sight.

She wasn't prepared to care, but she did.

CHAOS SURROUNDED them. But Blake wasn't entirely unfamiliar with that kind of situation. And apparently, from Anne's reaction, neither was she.

He could tell that the whole thing bothered her, though. Obviously, she was concerned for her mother. The woman had come around several minutes after they'd found her. And despite the situation, had begun issuing edicts immediately. Blood dripping and all.

Anne ignored her. He had to give her credit for fortitude. He was certain many people with less spine had simply caved in the face of her mother's tenacious and overbearing manner.

Everyone in the household was awake, the staff, the family, the guests. They milled about at the edges, not offering assistance, but refusing to leave. He supposed they wanted to see the spectacle. Or determine whether the old bat would live or die.

The paramedics had arrived within minutes. They'd evaluated Marie and were currently loading her onto a gurney. Anne, having—along with him—thrown on some clothes while they waited, walked behind the paramedics as they wheeled Marie out into the cold night. Red lights flashed eerily off the pale stone side of the house bathing everything in a deep pink color that reminded him of the blood still spattered across the rug in the other room.

Blake stayed immediately behind Anne. He wasn't about to let her out of his sight. Not now. Not when she might need him.

Several people followed them. Anne's aunt let out a dramatic wail and turned her face into one of her sons' shoulders. He'd seen better acting at his niece's kindergarten play.

The paramedics spoke to each other, to Marie and then to Anne. He paid little attention to the conversation, instead watching the small knot of people around them. The hairs on the back of his neck were standing on end again. Something had his instincts on red alert.

But Anne certainly snagged his attention when her raised voice cut through the dull roar of murmurs around them.

"No. I'm going."

"Ma'am, it's against regulations...."

"You tell that to your boss tomorrow when I call and explain how unaccommodating to the Prescott family you were."

The two paramedics shot each other a look. Before they could say anything, Blake moved in to defuse the situation.

"Anne, you can't go with her. I'll take you to the hospital. We'll be right behind her. I promise."

She didn't even spare him a glance, instead continuing her tenacious argument. He'd never seen her in full-on Prescott mode. It was slightly scary.

"I will sit up front and won't get in the way, but I'm not leaving my mother. Not now."

The woman in front of him was formidable. Not that his Anne wasn't, as well. He wouldn't want to get on the bad side of either of them. But this was an unapologetic trading on her family name, something his Anne would never do. And then he thought of the strings she'd pulled for his sister's wedding. Or maybe only for the people she cared about.

He glanced at the woman lying on the gurney in the center of the ambulance. Three minutes ago he wouldn't have listed Anne's mother among those she particularly cared about—and he hadn't blamed her.

Not that it mattered—Anne couldn't ride in the ambulance.

"Anne." He tugged on her arm, forcing her to look at him, see him and hear him. "Someone tried to abduct you less than twelve hours ago. You can't go with your mother, because there isn't enough room for me."

He watched as she processed the information. The acid that had started churning in his stomach slowly began to subside. She was intelligent. She'd realize he was right.

Instead, she jerked her arm out of his hold, walked quickly to the cab of the ambulance and climbed inside, not waiting for anyone to give her permission.

The paramedics shrugged, one quickly climbing into the back to make sure Marie was still stable, the other moving to the driver's side.

"What hospital?" Blake shouted.

"Winthrop."

Before they'd even pulled out of the driveway, Blake was racing for the garage he'd seen around the back of the house. George was quickly on his heels. "I'll drive you, Mr. Mitchell."

"Are you willing to break the law to get there?" Blake looked across at the other man, not slowing his sprint at all. He could see the pinched lines of worry across George's face, the brackets of pain at the sides of his mouth.

"Absolutely."

ANNE COULDN'T catch her breath. She could hear the beeps and other sounds from the back of the ambulance as the paramedic worked on her mother. While Marie had looked fairly stable, Anne didn't understand the jargon the paramedic was speaking into a radio and that scared her. Maybe she'd lost consciousness again. Maybe she was worse than they'd thought. Maybe the only immediate family Anne had left was dying.

In all her years, she'd never thought that prospect would bother her.

When she'd walked in and found her brother dead in their hotel suite, she'd thought her world was collapsing around her. And now it was happening again. With Michael it had been a shock because he'd been so young. With her mother it was a shock because Anne never would have thought she'd care if Marie died.

She was losing her and for the briefest moment she allowed herself to panic. Without Marie, she'd have no one.

Blake. Why did her racing mind automatically turn to Blake? Because she could so easily see him becoming important in her life. And she wasn't ready for that, wasn't ready to leave herself open and vulnerable.

She knew he was angry with her, had seen the anxious and unhappy look in his eyes. He'd get over it. And if he didn't...well then maybe that was better.

Before she knew it, they were pulling up to the bay of the emergency room.

"Stay out of the way." The paramedic threw the words at her as he jumped from the cab.

She slipped out, plastering her body against the door so as not to cause a problem. She got a brief glimpse of her mother as they wheeled her past.

Her eyes were closed but she didn't appear to be unconscious. Her body didn't have the limp and broken look that it'd had earlier. Marie had simply closed her eyes. In pain? To avoid looking at Anne?

The doors to the hospital swished open on a blast of warm air and the sighing sound of an airlock releasing. At the same moment, the discordant squeal of tires ripped through the night. Anne automatically turned, pushing her body hard against the cold metal at her back. Damn, she was jumpy these days. Not that she didn't have good reason to be. But she hated not feeling safe. She'd fought hard to make a secure and peaceful life for herself.

A frown pulled at her lips as she realized it was just George, with Blake sitting in the front seat glaring through the windshield at her.

Turning away, she followed the men rushing her mother's gurney into the hospital.

A long hall greeted them, and a group of people, as well. She gathered they were nurses and doctors who'd been waiting for her mother to arrive. The paramedic said something and one of them glanced in her direction.

A woman peeled off from the group, coming to a complete stop just as Anne reached her. She grasped onto Anne's arm, pulling her up short.

"Ms. Prescott, you'll have to wait here. We'll let you know what's going on as soon as the doctors have taken a look at your mother."

She was about to protest when another set of arms circled her waist. She didn't have to look to know it was Blake. The cells of her body reacted to him in an ancient and baffling way, almost as if his presence changed her makeup at the most elemental level.

A small part of the tension that had strung her tight and kept her going began to leak out.

"You'll only get in the way," he whispered into her ear, leaning close. "We'll find a nice, quiet corner and wait. Together."

The panic and pain didn't hit until that moment and then she was eternally grateful for his presence. For the strength he gave her.

She didn't need him. She would have been fine without him. But it would be so much easier with him there.

13

"WHAT THE HELL did you think you were doing?"

Once the nurse showed them to a small, more private, waiting area off a long corridor, Blake turned on Anne. He knew now wasn't the time, but the fear was still washing through his body.

She'd put herself in danger and there was nothing he could do to stop her. He needed a release for the dread and anger or he was going to explode.

Considering where they were, his choices were fighting it out with Anne or punching his hand through a wall, because what he really wanted to do—drop her to the floor and drive deep inside her—wasn't an option.

So they would have the conversation. Blake forcefully lowered his voice, trying to find a calm that he didn't feel. "Why did you do that?"

She looked up at him, her eyes lost and his chest clenched. Crap.

"I couldn't let her go alone. She needed someone and I couldn't turn my back on her." He recognized the parallels she was drawing between this and her brother. She hadn't been there for Michael, so she was determined to be there for her mother even if the woman didn't deserve the loyalty.

Anger and frustration drained slowly from his body as if the expression on Anne's face had pulled a plug that had been holding the emotions inside. The fear didn't go anywhere, though, because the danger was still very real. If something had happened to her...

"I know. But you can't do things like that, Anne. You can't just run off without protection. Someone out there is trying to hurt you. You have to think of yourself, too."

"I seriously doubt the paramedics wanted to hurt me."

He took a single, calming breath. "Probably not, but what if I hadn't gotten here right away? What if whoever wants to hurt you had? You would have been an easy target in the chaos."

The vacant expression slowly left her eyes, replaced by a weak imitation of the drive and passion that usually lit her from within. "Do you want me to live my life afraid of every shadow?"

"No. But I was hired to protect you. Let me do my job."

She didn't need to know that he had no intention of taking anyone's money. Especially if it made her more compliant.

"Would it help if I fired you?" She cocked an eyebrow at him, the smooth blond arch making the unease in his chest lessen just a bit. She was returning to some semblance of her normal self.

"You can't. Besides, I wouldn't leave." He reached across the space that separated them and pulled her into his arms. "I'm not going anywhere. My sister would never forgive me if something happened to you."

It was a lame attempt to make Anne smile. Only, he was quickly realizing that he was the one who wouldn't be able to live if something happened to her. But he wasn't ready to say that out loud, and she wasn't ready to hear it. He didn't want to give her a reason to push him away and leave herself vulnerable. And she would. What they had was messy and the Anne he knew didn't like messy.

As much as she pretended not to have anything of her mother in her, she sought out order and demanded control from everything in her world. Her house was spotless. Her life was clear of complicated relationships....

She'd lived with chaos for many years before she ran away, so he couldn't blame her for wanting a bit of peace. But he refused to let her need for control trigger their separation and her headlong rush toward danger.

He tucked her head beneath his chin, pressed his lips against her hair, and told her a small part of the truth, something she might be able to handle. "I'd never be able to forgive myself if something happened to you."

If she chose to believe it was because he couldn't handle any more guilt, that was fine. The real reason was that he'd fallen in love with her.

Her shoulders rose and fell on a sigh. He wasn't sure if it was one of relief or concern. She rolled her head, burying her nose into his chest. But her arms didn't come around him; she just stood there, using him as a wall to prop herself up.

"Why don't we sit down?"

She nodded and followed him quietly to the chairs in the corner.

A couple hours later the room was quiet. They'd been at the hospital for a while; Blake would guess it was about four in the morning. They were alone, no one else had come into the waiting area since they'd arrived. The Prescott name certainly came with perks. Not that that mattered to him.

It was easier this way for Anne, though. She didn't have to listen to crying babies, sick and upset. Or the coughs and sneezes of the normal waiting room crowd.

In fact, she'd finally closed her eyes and gone to sleep about fifteen minutes earlier. He'd turned the light off and convinced her to lie across the bench and put her head in his lap.

He didn't like the way her eyes looked, deep dark circles bruising the skin beneath. She was exhausted and fighting against an emotional barrage even he couldn't begin to guess at.

His hand went automatically to her forehead, stroking the stray strands of hair back from her face. She hadn't taken the time to brush it as they'd waited for the ambulance to arrive. It was still rumpled and knotted from their night together. Not that anyone else would notice. Only he knew she hadn't been tucked into bed and fast asleep.

Their earlier conversation played through his head. Not the specific words but rather the emotions that had ripped through him at lightning speed. Frustration, fear, anxiety.

The moment that ambulance door closed behind Anne... He'd never been so scared in his life.

It wasn't a pleasant feeling. Not one he was used to. Not one he ever wanted to experience again.

Anne had become an integral part of his life in such a short time. She was willful and confident and beautiful and strong. Stronger than even she was aware. He admired her for the way she'd built a new life for herself, using nothing more than her principles, determination and inability to accept the word *no*. Not many people— especially those with the kind of silver spoon she'd had in her mouth—would be able to turn their backs on everything for a harder life.

He could sympathize. Isn't that exactly what he'd done when he'd gone after Karyn's rapist? He'd known the consequences for what he was doing and had willingly paid the price. There were easier ways, ways that wouldn't have crashed his life and career just as he'd been starting to build them.

But they hadn't been right. Karyn had needed a protector; the other women the lowlife would have hurt needed a protector. To his mind, at least, it had been the right thing to do. And he hadn't hesitated.

Just as leaving behind the money, fame and easy life had been the right decision for Anne. At the time.

But now? Now, he was seriously afraid her place was here, with her mother and the family business. He knew she was going to stay and he couldn't ask her not to. He'd watched her yesterday in the office, handling the business of running a multibillion-dollar corporation. She'd taken to it like a duck to water. She belonged there. She deserved the chance to succeed in her family's legacy.

It would have been difficult enough trying to manage a relationship with his business in Mississippi and her life in Birmingham. He'd already been away from Mitchell Security for too long. Yes, he had competent people, but the business was his to run. He couldn't put that responsibility off indefinitely. Not even for Anne.

Eventually he'd have to leave. The fear that thought brought on made his chest ache again. Rubbing a hand absently across his breastbone, he decided he didn't have to think about that now. He wasn't going anywhere today.

He needed to get away for a minute, though. Now, before she woke up and looked at him with those half-lidded, sleepy eyes and he did something he shouldn't, like grab on and never let go.

Blake gently lifted Anne's head, scooting to the side and rolling his jacket as a pillow. He stood for a moment, staring down at her. Her face was smooth and easy. In sleep she seemed contented, more so than he'd seen her since the night of Karyn's wedding. That night the alcohol had loosened her normal wariness.

Tonight, it had simply been exhaustion—and, he hoped in some part, his presence—that had brought her the same fleeting peace.

Shaking his head, he turned away, stopping to ask a nurse to keep an eye on her. The vending machines were only a few feet down the hall and he hadn't seen anyone in over an hour. The corridor was quiet.

Just as he slipped into the hallway the nurse appeared before him. "Mrs. Prescott is awake. You can go in to see her now."

His first instinct was to turn around and get Anne. But as the image of her finally peaceful and sleeping swam back into his mind he decided that maybe he'd go in first. If Marie was too drugged and out of it to talk then there was really no reason to wake Anne up.

Nodding, he followed the nurse down a series of cor-ridors and through the heavy hospital room door. It was far from the accommodations that Marie Prescott was used to, although he had no doubt she'd fix that as soon as humanly possible. He wondered if Winthrop had a suite. If not she'd probably have one built.

Her skin was pale, her body frail, but she was propped

high against a bank of pillows. Somehow, even this close to death's door, she still managed to look regal and in control of everything. Her eyes were open, although they appeared slightly glassy. Probably from the drugs they were pumping into her body through the needle taped to her arm.

"Mrs. Prescott."

Her gaze swung to him, slow and without her normal snap.

Despite that, her voice still managed to command. "Sit."

He complied. There was no reason not to.

"Where's Annemarie?"

"Asleep in the waiting room. I thought I'd let her rest while she could."

She nodded. For the first time Blake noticed a cross tattooed into the center of her forehead. There was a joke there—something about the devil and a religious tattoo—but now was not the time.

"What's with the cross?"

A discontented expression flashed across her face before she answered. "It's for the radiation. They use it as a target for the treatment."

He realized that the gaudy sapphire she'd been walking around with had hidden the mark from everyone. He imagined few people knew the truth. He wondered if Anne did.

Probably not. Just another example of the duplicity and secrets that seemed to permeate the family.

"She's turned into a fine young woman. It was touch and go there for a while but at least I don't have to clean up her messes anymore. Not like Michael. That last night…damn him for what he made me do." Her words trailed off for a moment and her eyes went almost vacant before she snapped back again. "She'll be fine. The company will be fine now that she's here."

For a minute Blake wondered why she was telling him these things, why she was talking to him at all. From the moment he'd met her Marie had treated him as if she wished he were invisible.

And then his focus sharpened on her actual words.

"What do you mean, 'what he made me do'?"

Her eyes blinked owlishly, her brain clearly trying to keep up with the thread of conversation. "Nothing. Nothing." Her hand waved the words away, but her movements were thick and heavy.

"What happened that night, Marie? What did Michael do?" What didn't Anne know?

"What did Michael do? He almost ruined this family, that's what he did. He almost made us a laughingstock." Despite the drug-induced lethargy, her words held weight and conviction.

"How? Anne told me that you and he fought that night. Over his choice of lifestyle."

"Oh, we fought all right. The boy didn't have any concern for the reputation of the family. He wouldn't listen to a word I said. In fact, even as I forbade him to see whoever was corrupting his mind, he turned his back on me and walked away. Walked right into the arms of that man and got himself killed."

Blake sat forward in his chair. "Killed? I thought he committed suicide. Anne found him. She told me."

As if realizing that she'd already said too much, Marie sank back into the thin hospital mattress, turned her gaze to the opposite wall and told him everything.

"He didn't kill himself. That man strangled him. During sex. Apparently, being gay wasn't enough for him. He had to let someone choke him to death."

Blake's eyes widened. That was not what he'd expected. He was grateful when she didn't wait for his reaction. What was the proper thing to say?

"I found him. In his room. Alone. Naked. A belt tight around his throat, facedown across his bed. I couldn't leave him there. I couldn't let the world know about his perversion…perversions.

"We moved him to the bathroom and staged the suicide."

Blake would find out who "we" was later.

"You disturbed a crime scene? How do you know he wanted the attention? How do you know it wasn't a murder?"

Her eyes finally fixed on him. "It was murder. And I know because he told me, that night, throwing it in my face that at least he'd found a way to be satisfied and happy. I knew as soon as I saw him what had happened. My one regret is that I didn't know who he'd been with so I had no idea who to ruin. In the end it really didn't matter. Michael was dead and I had the family reputation to think of. A murder investigation would have brought everything into the public eye. It was better this way."

Better for whom? He'd seen the years of pent-up grief and guilt that Anne dealt with over Michael's death. Over her refusal to come to him when he'd called.

"Who did you expect to find him?"

"Annemarie. She was the only one who hadn't witnessed the real scene and wouldn't be lying with her reaction when the police arrived. It had to be her."

Disgust rolled around inside him, like a snake chasing its tail.

"You set her up to find her dead brother? You

wanted her to walk in on that? What kind of mother are you?"

"Not a very good one."

At least they agreed on something.

"You have to tell her."

"No. I don't."

Oh, but she did. And he had no problem making sure she would do the right thing. The right thing for Anne.

"If you don't tell her when you get home, I will."

Disgusted at the depths Anne's mother had sunk to, Blake pushed up from the chair and walked away. He was five strides down the hallway when Peter rushed past.

He hadn't spent much time with the other man, but there was something about the way he stood at the edges of every group, silent and apart, that troubled Blake. Peter seemed to have the ability to make himself disappear. As someone who'd been trained in similar observation techniques, it bothered Blake. But was it unintentional or something Peter used to watch, measure and remember?

There was more, though. Something that niggled in the back of his mind. Always one to follow instincts, he turned to watch Peter as the man rushed into Marie Prescott's room, his words loud and clear.

"Marie! Are you all right?"

In that exact moment, Blake realized what had caught his attention. As Peter reached for the sill of the open doorway, the glint of a very expensive, very distinctive gold watch flashed on his wrist.

Blake had seen it before. Wrapped around Anne's throat as someone tried to pull her away from him.

He spun on his heel, heading back to the room. He'd

beat the hell out of the man. And then, if the creep could still talk, ask him why. Why would he do something like this?

But Anne's hand on his shoulder stopped him. "Blake?"

He looked back into her bleary eyes. She had a crease across her cheek from the folds of his jacket and there were dark circles under her eyes.

She'd been through so much already tonight. The last thing he wanted was to add to her stress.

Before he could decide what to do, Peter emerged from Marie's room and headed toward them.

"Peter. I didn't know you were here." Anne stepped up beside Blake, placing her hand on his arm in a casual gesture. It was a good thing, too, because he was fighting the urge to sock the asshole in the jaw.

"I just heard. Got here as fast as I could." With a half-apologetic smile he continued, "Marie asked me to handle a couple things for her. I'll be back in a few hours."

The man breezed away, but it didn't escape Blake's notice when he looked back over his shoulder at them.

"You know, I feel sorry for him. No doubt she has him waking up her oncologists and calling in every favor she can think of in order to get into a private hospital with catered meals. She says jump, he's always asked how high."

Shaking her head, Anne focused her gaze on the muted light spilling from the open doorway down the hall. "How is she?"

But Blake's brain was still processing her words. Peter didn't make a move without Marie's order? The thoughts that were forming were not pleasant but considering what he knew of Anne's mother… No, he wouldn't put anything past her.

"Blake?" Anne was looking at him with panic in her eyes. "What aren't you telling me?"

He realized he'd been staring a hole into the wall behind her head instead of answering her question. Idiot.

"She's fine. Drugged and a little loopy but she seems to be okay."

They moved to the open doorway and looked inside. Marie was asleep, burrowed into the pillows and thin blanket that covered her. Just as well. At the moment he had no idea what he would have said to the bitch.

Leading Anne away from the door, he said, "Why don't we go back to the estate? She's asleep now and probably will be for hours. You need to sleep, too, on something more comfortable than a waiting room chair."

And he needed to figure out what to do next.

14

BLAKE HAD BEEN WATCHING for the past twenty-four hours as Anne marshaled the staff around her, barking like a general. She'd seamlessly taken her mother's place as head of both the household and the corporation.

She had more of Marie in her than she probably knew—the good qualities anyway.

While he'd spent a large chunk of his time trailing behind Anne and making sure she was in no immediate danger, he'd also managed a little digging.

From what he could gather, Peter had been Marie's personal assistant for at least nine years. He'd been treated almost as one of the family during that time. And Blake wasn't sure being part of the family was a good thing, not after what he'd learned about Marie.

The question of what the man wanted remained. And was he operating under his own directive or Marie's? Blake hadn't seen him since the hospital so he'd had little opportunity to find out. His gut told him that Peter, Marie and recent events were all linked.

Something about the whole situation reeked. By her own admission, Marie had gone to great lengths to protect her idea of what the family should be. And he had firsthand knowledge of how ruthless she could be when she wanted something.

Anne herself had said, during their first conversation at her town house, that her mother had been pestering her for months to come home. What would she do? Or maybe the better question was what *wouldn't* she do to get what she wanted?

Very little, Blake thought.

There were three things that kept him from whisking Anne away immediately. First, he didn't think she'd go, not with her mother as sick as she was.

Second, in looking back on everything that had happened, he realized Anne hadn't really been in any danger. The break-in had been while she was at work and nothing had been taken. The shot in the parking lot had gone way wide, and the shooter had been plenty close enough to hit her if he'd wanted to. And the abduction attempt, while scary at the time, hadn't had much chance of success considering he'd been a few steps away. Anyone worth his salt would have taken Blake out first and then gone after Anne. If his true intention had been to kidnap her.

But what if the goal had been to scare her?

He needed more than a hunch to bring to Anne. Or to convince himself that she was safe. The whole situation would be enough to send her into a tailspin. It might even send her running.

Was he keeping the information from her because he thought it was the right thing to do or because he was afraid her reaction would include shutting him out along with everyone else?

No, he honestly thought that the confession needed to come from Marie and not him.

Besides, they'd both been a little preoccupied.

Marie was coming home tonight, though. And while part of him worried she wasn't up to the strain of a soul-baring confession, a larger part feared she might not ever get another chance. From speaking with Anne he knew Marie didn't have much time. The radiation wasn't working and the tumor had actually grown. Originally they'd given her a few months. They'd brought that down to maybe sixty days if she was lucky.

He figured if they felt she was strong enough to come home, this was probably the best opportunity. She wasn't going to get any better and Anne needed to hear the truth before it was too late.

"We have some time before the hordes descend."

She startled him out of his thoughts, but the moment her arms wrapped around his waist and her body pressed full length against his he knew he'd been aware of her at all times. His body certainly had.

He recognized that she was using him as an outlet. An outlet for the pent-up emotions she hadn't yet been able to face. Guilt, frustration, fear, anger… Passion was an easy channel and he was convenient. He knew he should push her away, deny them both, and force her to recognize that what they had together was far from convenient.

It was messy and had the potential to be very painful. But it was real.

But his body wouldn't let him. It seemed to have a mind of its own.

"At some point, this is going to have to stop." He whispered the words against her skin as his mouth trailed down the arch of her neck.

"I know. When are you leaving?"

Blake pulled back, shaking his head. "That's—" Her mouth cut his words off. By the time they both came up for air he'd forgotten what he'd been saying. The fuzzy part of his brain that still functioned knew it was important, but the desire that sizzled through his blood said it wasn't important enough.

She attacked him with a passion that flashed high and burned quickly. Their clothes melted away, slithering to the floor with nothing more than a thought and a caress. Her hands were everywhere, her hot mouth a brand to his skin.

She was his own private tigress, a raw, intense animal that he matched step for step. It was instinct, as if his body knew he must meet her wild side or fall beneath the sharp bite of her need.

But there was something missing. Something that had slipped away after what they'd shared in the shower, when she'd been so open and bare to him.

Tonight he was determined to recapture the connection, to turn their time together from mind-blowing sex and back to that elemental bond.

Grasping her wrists in both hands, Blake flattened her palms to his chest and stilled her tantalizing touches.

Taking three short steps back, he pulled her with him into the lone patch of early moonlight that fell through the window of the room they'd been sharing—his room. She'd refused to let him back into her bed after that first night. Another way she was placing emotional wedges between them.

A glint of power and arousal sparked in her eyes and a teasing smile curled the corners of her lips. Pressing her body against his, she allowed him to keep control of her hands and used the slip and slide of her naked body to arouse him.

Damn how it worked.

But this was too important for distraction.

They might not have everything worked out, but he'd be damned if he'd let her take what they did have and twist it.

After a moment, she seemed to realize he was holding himself away from her—not physically but mentally. He'd waited for that moment, knowing she'd come easier if he didn't force her.

"Blake?"

She tried to pull away, a gentle tug on his hold of her wrists. When he wouldn't let go, she pulled harder. He let this play out as well, until she stood still.

Their bodies touched, not as closely as before but somehow it was almost worse as the bend of her elbows kept everything but the tip of her breasts and the head of his erection away.

The sensation was torturous. He knew they both wanted more. Need pounded at the back of his brain, a tribal tattoo ringing against centuries of the masculine urge to claim what was his, to possess and conquer and dominate.

But that wouldn't win him this woman.

People had been trying to dominate and conquer and possess Anne her whole life. He needed to be different.

Her eyes darted about, landing on the wall of windows behind them, the rug at their feet, his chin, cheeks and forehead. Finally, when her gaze met his he knew he had her.

She couldn't look away.

This he understood. It was the same for him. The moment she entered a room it was as if no one else existed. It had been that way from the first moment he'd seen her and had never changed. Even when he'd tried to ignore the connection between them, it had been there like his own personal gravity, drawing him toward her.

He looked deep into her eyes, trying to convey everything he felt. He knew it was too early to voice the words—she still wasn't ready to hear them. But maybe the more he showed her he loved her, the more she'd realize he meant the words with every fiber of his being.

"Blake?" This time his name trembled on her lips. Gone was his fearless temptress, his corporate wizard, the woman who could handle absolutely any problem that landed in her lap. Instead the vulnerable woman she hid beneath those veneers looked back. The real woman.

The woman he loved.

His heart stuttered with fear and uncertainty. He wanted Anne in his life for as long as she'd have him. But what if something happened to her? What if he couldn't have her?

The vulnerability that love created almost sent him to his knees. He was used to having control over every aspect of his life.

What if things went badly? He wasn't sure he'd recover.

When the uncertainty in Anne's eyes flipped to a blank mask he knew fear had made him wait one second too long. That change in her was all the catalyst he needed. She was worth any risk—physical, mental or emotional. He'd take what he could get and be grateful for it.

"Don't. Don't hide from me." He leaned into her, holding her gaze as he brought their lips, their bodies, their souls together.

"I do not need a sex kitten, Anne. I want you. The real you."

In one swift motion, she ripped her hands from his hold. He had a brief moment to wonder if he'd pushed her too far. But before he could do anything about it, she shoved at his shoulders, the surprise and momentum forcing him back.

His body smacked against the icy window and he sucked in a breath at the shock of cold glass against his bare skin.

"Every man wants a sex kitten."

"Don't get me wrong, I like aggressive, especially on you, but I don't want you to play a role with me. I don't need Annemarie Prescott, wanton, hedonistic exhibitionist."

That tempting, knowing smile curled at her lips again, and his libido raced and his erection pulsed.

Her hand snaked down, wrapping around his cock and squeezing tight. "What *do* you need then?"

Her voice was sultry, her eyes seductive, but the words were wrong. Even as her hand flexed around him, his body ached to just let it go. Was it really that important that he break her now?

Wrapping his own hand around her fist, he stilled her motions. "I need you to at least admit this is real. To admit that this matters…to you."

Her thumb brushed against the base of his cock, a stroke that was both heaven and hell—temptation and torture. But he refused to give in.

Blake stared into her eyes and knew the moment something shifted. Oh, desire and hunger still glowed deep there, raw and real, but now there was something else. Something even more powerful and awe inspiring.

Her voice and face gentled and with her free hand she reached for him, cupping her palm around his face. "Right now, you're the only thing that's good in my life. I don't know what I would have done without you."

She brought their bodies together, joining her mouth with his in a timeless way that made his chest ache. Whispering against his lips, she said, "I need you. Please don't leave me here alone."

It wasn't lost on him that she'd made the admission in a way that meant she hadn't had to look him in the eye while she said it. She was still protecting herself, but he'd give her that. She'd taken the first step and today that was all he could ask of her.

Grabbing her waist, he lifted her off the floor and spun so her back connected with the winter-kissed glass.

Her own breath hissed out into the curve of his neck, hot in contrast to the chill still covering his spine.

And there was something about the contrast that spiked the heat between them even higher. Almost as if the disparity made him appreciate the warmth of their bodies even more.

In one quick thrust he sheathed himself inside the burning heat of her sex. This time her breath leaked out on a groan of pleasure and satisfaction.

Her legs wrapped around his waist, one arm locking her body with his, the other searching aimlessly for something solid to anchor to.

Her fingers slid noisily against the glass at her back, searching for purchase that wasn't there. He braced her against the cool, smooth surface and couldn't hold back.

He thrust in and out, in a pulse-pounding rhythm

that stole his breath and shattered his senses. She was so warm and whole.

He could spend every waking moment of his life locked here, tight inside her body.

Even as her cries built between them, from murmurs to begging to screams for release, he could hear the scrabble of her fingernails against the window. Her body pulsed around him, swelling to hold him tighter, coaxing him closer and closer to the edge. Just as he thought he'd lose the fight, the ripples of his release starting deep at the center of his spine, she erupted around him. A bucking, throbbing explosion of pleasure and pressure.

Letting go of his own release, he welcomed the oblivion of sensation. Even as his muscles quivered with the power of his orgasm he realized he wasn't going to be able to hold them up anymore. Grasping her, he rolled them both to the floor.

The ripping sound took several seconds to penetrate his sex-fogged brain, but as the gauzy material floated down around them, covering them in a film of ethereal white he realized what had happened.

They'd ripped down the curtains.

Anne laughed, rolling to the floor beside him and holding the material away from them with straight arms.

She turned to Blake, her eyes clear and warm, raw with spent desire for him.

"Marie is going to kill us."

She laughed again—the sound had an edge that made him tense. "If the cancer doesn't kill her first." Anne's laughter bubbled over, turning into tears with no warning. One minute she was staring at him with satisfaction in her eyes, the next those eyes were awash with anguish he felt echo through his own soul.

He did not like seeing her in pain.

Pain that was amplified because she hadn't expected it and in some corner of her mind he knew she didn't want it. Which just added guilt to the mix.

Reaching for her, he gathered her into his arms, rolling them together into the cocoon of draperies. Their breath mingled together in the damp closeness as she buried her head in the crook of his shoulder.

"Everything's going to be fine, Annie." He rubbed her back rhythmically as he told her something he was very afraid would turn into a lie.

Her mother was dying. Her world was crashing down around her ears. And he wanted to pull a Neanderthal move, throw her over his shoulder and whisk her away to some deep, dark cave where they could shut everyone out and always be together.

"How can you know that?" Her words were wet with the tears that still tracked down her face. The tears were silent now, the gentle release of her anguish. It meant a lot that she felt safe enough with him to let them go.

"I can't save her. I can't change this," she said. "And I can't run away and pretend it isn't happening. I don't want to stay here but I know I'm going to. The company needs someone at the helm and as much as I want to hate her…I can't while she's dying. So I'm going to give her this last wish because it's the only thing I can do."

"I know." Blake would have expected nothing less from her. It was amazing to him that she'd become such a warm and loving woman considering the cold environment she'd been raised in. She really was an argument for nature over nurture.

"But I don't want to leave my life in Birmingham," Anne continued. "I don't want to give up that woman I fought so hard to find."

He grasped her chin and turned her to look at him. Her green eyes were luminous with the soft sheen of tears still clinging to her lashes. "Then don't. You might have needed to get away from here in order to find the woman you wanted to be but you've found her. She's intelligent, sensual—" he couldn't stop himself from stroking a finger down her spine just so he could watch her arch into the touch "—kind, loyal, fiercely protective of those she loves, not to mention a force to be reckoned with when riled up.

"Anne, running away didn't make you anything you weren't already. It just helped you shed things that were holding you back. You know what's important now. And I have no doubt that you'll succeed at everything you do…including running Prescott Hotels."

She was silent for several moments, her eyes drifting down to the center of his chest in an absent perusal that spoke of her familiarity with his body. Her finger followed, the smooth pad and sharp nail drifting languidly across his chest. Her body eased against him, losing the hard edge of muscles pulled tight. He enjoyed seeing her relax, liked that he could help calm her mind. At least he could do that.

But then her gaze traveled back up to his, her eyes locking with his own. The anguish was still there, only something about it had changed.

He didn't understand what until she said, "But I don't want to lose you."

PETER LET his head fall back against the wall. They were in there together. He knew because he'd watched them disappear, could still hear the echo of their lovemaking ringing in his ears.

He'd been trying to find Annemarie alone all day but

between Mitchell shadowing her every move and the household's uproar over Marie's accident, Annemarie hadn't been alone for five seconds, much less the amount of time he'd need to begin her instruction as his mate.

Frustration was a constant companion. The bad news from Marie's doctors was going to require that he speed up the timetable he'd laid out to woo Annemarie. They no longer had the luxury of her coming to the conclusion of their perfection on her own.

He would have to show her.

"There you are. Mrs. Prescott has just arrived home and requested to see you in her study."

Peter didn't appreciate the tone of voice the chauffer used or his hard-eyed look. George would definitely be one of the first to find that with the changing of the guard came a change in the staff.

With one final look over his shoulder toward Mitchell's closed door, Peter set off at a fast clip through the house. The sooner he took care of whatever Marie wanted, the sooner he could return to waiting for an opportunity to get Annemarie alone.

Stopping before the doorway, Peter hunched his shoulders slightly and put on a subservient expression before shuffling into the room. "You wanted to see me?"

"Come in and shut the door." Peter did as he was told, what was expected.

She was propped up in one of the armchairs and while she still maintained the air of authority and strength that had always been her hallmark, there was no mistaking that she was very ill.

"I received some rather startling news."

"I'm so sorry. How long did they give you?"

From the very beginning Marie had been candid with

him about her diagnosis, so he wasn't surprised that she wished to discuss her impending end and the details that might involve.

"No, not from my doctors." She waited a beat, purposely drawing out the moment for some effect that he didn't understand. He'd seen her do it numerous times, as he stood silently at her elbow. He did not like being on the receiving end of that pregnant pause. "From Blake Mitchell."

"Oh?" What could the man have told her?

"He informed me that not only was Anne shot at before she left Birmingham, but there was also an attempted kidnapping the day she went to the office."

"You told me to convince her to stay."

Her eyes hardened within her wizened face. Her body might be revolting but her brain was certainly sharp enough. "I told you to scare her, not try to abduct her."

"You weren't specific with your instructions. I did what I thought best."

"Well, you thought wrong. I never wanted my daughter in any real danger."

His jaw tightened. Despite mentally telling them not to, he felt his shoulders straightening. "She wasn't."

He heard his own voice, sharp and impatient. How dare she question his decisions in carrying out her orders? She never had before and he'd given her no reason to start now.

"Peter, I've given you everything over the years. A home, clothes, servants, even a position as my personal assistant."

"And I've done everything you've asked of me." And kept his mouth shut about those things she'd required him to do.

"You've overstepped your bounds this time. You went too far with Annemarie. I want you to pack your things and be gone by morning."

No! Peter stumbled, knocked off balance by what she'd just said. "What?" How could she do this?

"Oh, don't worry. George will provide you with a checking account. I'll make sure money continues to be deposited every month. I promised your mother I would take care of you and I never go back on my word."

Oh no. Hell no. He wasn't leaving here with nothing more than an allowance. No, not when he'd worked so hard in order to have it all.

"You can't throw me out. You can't fire me."

Marie's eyes narrowed. "Oh, I guarantee you I can."

"I know too much. The first thing I'm going to do is run to the nearest tabloid and spill my guts."

"Go ahead. Not only will that checking account I mentioned run dry, but you'll find the betrayal of my secrets won't get you far. I may have done some bad things, but then so have you. And I'll be dead in two months. Not much can happen to me after that."

Impotent rage built in his belly, a burning mass of anger, rejection, disappointment and frustration. He wouldn't let her do this.

A satisfied gleam in her eyes, Marie sat back in her chair. "You haven't a leg to stand on, my boy. Run along and lick your wounds alone. I find I don't care to watch."

Peter's hands balled into tight fists. He stepped toward Marie, his rage washing everything, including her precious sapphire, a sickly red. He wanted to choke the life out of her, just as he'd choked her son. Only this time, anger was the driver, not passion.

He took another step forward, his momentum stopped only when George materialized at her side. He hadn't heard the man but should have known—Marie always went into battle with reinforcements. Until five minutes ago, that job had been his.

Whirling away, he stormed from the room. She'd banished him. Thrown him out like so much trash. She'd been alone after Annemarie left. Alone except for him. He'd given her his whole life, sold his soul to the devil. He deserved riches and fame, everything being a Prescott would bring.

Surely there was still some way to get what he deserved….

Slamming through the house, he went into his bedroom. He wasn't in the servants' quarters, but he might as well be. The room he'd been given when he'd arrived here as a child hadn't changed. Decorated in impersonal blue, red and white stripes, it could have been anyone's.

Jerking the closet doors open, Peter grabbed a suitcase, knowing that Marie was a woman of her word and would have security at his door within the hour. As he pulled the suitcase out, a black plastic box that had been stacked behind it toppled over, settling at his feet.

The gun. The one he'd used in Birmingham to scare Annemarie. He stared at it, his anger bleeding off, leaving behind nothing but determination.

If he couldn't have what he wanted, then he'd make sure Marie couldn't, either. He'd make her pay. He'd make them all pay for thinking he didn't belong, for using him up and spitting him out.

Marie had already lost her son. Perhaps it was time to take her last hope, her daughter, as well.

And while he was at it, he'd take Mitchell out, too.

The bastard had cost him everything. It would be the perfect setup. He could see the headlines now: Jealous Boyfriend with Prior Conviction Murders Prescott Heiress.

It would be perfect.

15

HER BODY SHOOK as she slipped back into the clothes she'd discarded earlier. Not from the force of their lovemaking but from the realization of what she'd just admitted. This thing with Blake had gotten out of hand. She'd lost all control over him, the situation, herself.

She'd done the impossible. She'd done the stupid. She'd let him become important. She'd fallen in love.

At the end of the day, it wouldn't matter. She couldn't keep him. He was like the puppy she'd brought home from the shelter when she'd visited with her class from the academy. Marie had immediately ordered him returned. No amount of crying or begging or screaming or wishing had changed the inevitable.

She'd known she wouldn't be able to keep him, but the warm, puppy-dog licks during the ride home in the limo had been worth it.

And so would her time with Blake.

It would hurt like hell when he left her. But she'd survive because she always did.

In the meantime, her mother had returned and was properly settled in her sitting room. It was time to face the lioness in her den. Anne had avoided the inevitable as long as possible. Fighting reluctance and the desire to turn around and go back to Blake, she walked the length of the house toward Marie's sanctuary. Her mother absently waved her to a wing chair as she entered the room.

Anne opened her mouth to begin the rundown of the company's situation—which was what she thought her mother would want—but Marie cut her off before she could start.

"There's something I need to tell you."

The twist in her mother's mouth told Anne that she might need to tell her something but she wasn't thrilled with the prospect of actually doing it. For some reason Anne wanted to save her mother the pain of saying the words aloud.

"I know. I spoke to the doctors." Anne took a deep breath. "And I'll stay. I'll take over the company. I can't promise that I'll keep it after you're gone…. I don't know what I'll do. But for now that's one less thing for you to worry about."

Marie stared across at her, silent for several seconds. Anne wondered what the woman was thinking. Was she gloating? Anne didn't think so, but with her mother it was always hard to tell. What she suddenly understood was it didn't matter. She had no control over her mother's reactions and expectations. She had to do what *she* felt was right. Not for Marie but for herself.

"I'm glad to hear it, but that wasn't what I wanted to talk to you about."

Anne's eyebrows flew up. "Oh?"

"It's about Michael. He…he didn't commit suicide."

BLAKE PAUSED outside the doorway and listened. He'd been looking for Anne—she'd slipped from the room when he'd taken the ruined draperies down to housekeeping. When George had told him she was with her mother, he'd known he needed to get there pronto. He'd intended to be with her, offering himself as an ally, when she faced Marie.

"What are you talking about?" Anne's voice, shrill and full of confusion made his insides cringe. As much as he knew she needed the truth, he also realized the information would devastate her. And the last thing he wanted was to see her in pain…more pain.

Without thinking, he pushed into the room. Both women glanced at him—Anne's eyes full of confusion, Marie's full of resentment.

"Your brother was murdered."

"What do you mean? How?" She looked to him, for understanding he didn't have, for answers that weren't his to give.

What he could give her was the support of his presence, the knowledge that no matter what, she wasn't alone. Not like after she'd found Michael.

Taking a step toward her, Blake stood at her back, offering his silent support and presence. With a distracted gesture, Anne reached behind and grasped his hand. "That can't be true."

Marie was cold and clinical, as if she were talking about the death of a fish instead of her son. "It is. He was strangled by his boyfriend. Apparently they choked each other for pleasure."

They could have all done without the dripping disdain, but Anne didn't seem to notice. Instead, she focused on the implications of the words themselves.

"Choked? Pleasure? I don't understand."

Marie's huff of unhappiness burst between them.

"They strangle each other. Something about the loss of oxygen increasing sexual satisfaction."

"That's not what I meant!" Anne's consternation rang out. "I meant I don't understand how this could have happened. How it could be the truth."

"Trust me, it's the truth." Marie's lips thinned into a hard line.

Anne stared at her.

"How do you know this?"

Blake hated to see her confusion. The world as she'd known it was changing before her eyes. How do you handle it when an event that has altered your life turns out to be a lie?

"He told me. That night during our fight. He taunted me, saying he'd found something that excited him, that gave him a sense of control and pleasure. And he told me there was nothing I could do to stop him."

The anger that twisted Marie's face made Blake want to slap some warmth and maternal instinct into her. But lurking beneath it all was a single spark of guilt that made him hope she actually did have some feelings for her daughter and her dead son, even if she didn't seem to know how to show it.

"But I found him. Dead. In the bathroom."

Marie's mouth warped with bitterness. "We moved him to the bathroom precisely so you would find him."

Then again, maybe not.

Anne's grip on his hand tightened to a painful level. Blake didn't say a word.

"What?"

"It had to be you. We needed your honest emotions so the police couldn't pick apart your story. Your genuine reaction was what we wanted the world to know."

Blake watched as Anne's back stiffened. He could

almost hear the wheels in her head spin as she processed the information, as she came to terms with this new reality.

"You…you would rather the world think Michael had been weak and depressed enough to kill himself than have them know he was gay?"

Marie's voice hardened and she stood up, an elegant queen speaking down to the masses. "My actions had nothing to do with his sexual…orientation. I didn't want the world to know about the perverted and unseemly way he happened to die, about the humiliation and degradation he sought for himself. He was gone. I was simply trying to retain as much of his dignity as I could."

"Bullshit." Anne leaned away from Blake, her words sharp and barbed as she aimed for her mother. "The only thing you've ever cared about is your own reputation. Not once in my entire life have you ever put what I wanted above your own desires. Not once did you do that for Michael. You didn't care one damn little bit about him. You've only ever cared about yourself."

Marie's fists clenched at her sides, impotent weapons she couldn't use to change the truth.

Leaning back against Blake, Anne let the silence swell for several seconds. "Why are you telling me this now? Why not just take the secret to your grave?"

Marie's eyes narrowed and zeroed in on Blake's face. For the first time he truly saw how empty and narcissistic she was. He had made her do something she hadn't wanted. And now he was about to pay.

"Ask him. I knew this would hurt you. He gave me no choice."

She made it sound as if she'd kept the information from Anne in order to protect her. Bitch.

Anne pulled away before slowly turning to face him.

He looked into her face and saw her emotional up-heaval. All he wanted to do was take her in his arms, hold her tight and promise her that they'd get through this together.

But the hand she held up between them prevented him from doing that.

"What is she talking about? You knew the truth? And you didn't tell me?"

"Yes." He saw the accusation and disappointment in her eyes and almost regretted the word. But he'd never lied to her and he had no intention of starting today.

"She needed to be the one to tell you, Anne. You needed to hear the truth from her."

"Bullshit."

He did not like having that word—one he'd whole-heartedly agreed with when it was aimed at her mother—thrown at him.

"You're just as bad as she is, protecting yourself. You just didn't want to be the one to tell me the truth."

"You're right. What we have is so precarious. You've been holding me at a distance for days, keeping me at arm's length even as you've let me into your bed. I was afraid. Afraid that telling you the truth would send you running away from me. Away from what we have."

"Well, now you'll never know, will you?"

Turning, she stalked toward the door. He reached for her, but she jerked her arm away.

"Don't touch me." Raking her heated gaze across both him and the silent woman standing in the corner, she said, "Both of you leave me alone."

Dropping his empty hand to his side, he let her walk away.

Maybe giving her a little time to cool down would help.

ANNE STORMED through the house, slamming doors and banging walls. She headed out through the back, past the guesthouse and pool to the sprawling, open grounds and the woods edging the property.

She was pissed. And hurt. And confused.

She needed to get some air and clear her head. She needed to be alone for five minutes so she could process how her life had just been tilted, shaken and rearranged—like a snow globe, only a hell of a lot less pretty.

What she'd always thought—the events that had shaped and molded the woman she now was—was a lie.

Now what?

That Blake had been involved in the discovery just muddied the waters. She was angry at him for keeping her mother's secret, no matter why he'd done it. But had it really been his place to tell her? She wasn't sure.

God, when had her life gotten so complicated? Part of her missed the simple days of her youth when her only goal had been to feel pleasure at any cost—oh, and to piss off her mother in the process. One goal, one outcome, no complications.

If she was honest with herself, she'd gone from one uncomplicated life to another. The life she'd built for herself in Alabama was simple in its own way. She had few personal connections, which meant she didn't have to worry about pleasing or upsetting someone else. Karyn had been the single exception to the rule, but they'd had the bond of secrets and emotional pain to unite them in understanding.

Here in New York she'd never opened herself up enough to let someone hurt her. Of course, Michael had already been there, inside her heart. They'd shared their own bond of understanding and comfort. They'd given to each other what their mother hadn't given them.

And when he left, she knew she couldn't handle it alone. That more than anything was what prompted her to run. She'd had no ally left in the wasteland her life had become.

But she'd simply run from one numb existence to another.

Until Blake had barged in.

He'd hacked his way into her life and heart. She hadn't wanted him there but there he was. And the thought of turning her back on him and walking away left her breathless with panic. The thought of trying to build a life together, of admitting her feelings for him and opening herself to the potential for pain and disappointment also left her scared, but not nearly as much as the prospect of twenty, thirty, fifty years without him.

He made her feel powerful, sensual, good and worthwhile. She didn't want to lose that.

She needed to talk to him, to take the risk that what they had could be something special. They were good for each other. He brought out the best in her and she challenged him and his overprotective-male complex.

She turned back toward the house, suddenly needing to find him more than her next breath, but she saw that she'd come farther than she'd thought. The moon was blotted out by the canopy of pines above her head. The house glowed like a white Tinkertoy in the distance. An unexpected shiver of unease rippled down her spine. The grounds were well lit, but very little light penetrated the forest.

She was out here alone. And while no one had tried to hurt her here on the estate, they still hadn't caught the person who wanted to harm her.

She wanted to kick herself for ordering Blake to leave her alone. But she knew he wouldn't have let her walk away if he'd thought she was in real danger.

Quickening her steps, she headed toward the house. Fifteen minutes at the most and she'd be back.

She could see the edge of the trees and part of her let out a silent sigh of relief…. Until a silhouette stepped into the path ahead of her.

She knew immediately it wasn't Blake and her heart sank to her toes. The man—and it was definitely a man—was too short and wide across the hips. His stance was all wrong.

Her steps faltered but there was nowhere for her to go. Nowhere to hide. Even the trees offered her little cover since the man was so close.

She couldn't see his face in the dim light. But as she walked slowly forward, one cautious step at a time, his features came into focus.

"Peter." And for about thirty seconds she was happy to see him. "You scared me. What are you doing out so far? I didn't even realize you were here."

"I'm always here. I've always been here. You've just never seen me."

His voice, accusatory and bitter, wiped away any thought that she'd escaped danger.

Anne instinctively knew she was looking into the face of the man who'd been making her life hell.

And no one knew where she was. She was too far away from the house for anyone to hear her if she screamed. He could do whatever he wanted.

As she stared at the man she'd always considered harmless she realized two things. One, he held a small black handgun close to his side, almost completely hidden in the murky light around them. And two, the only thing she'd ever regret was not telling Blake how much she loved him.

"Why are you doing this?"

Anne watched with trepidation as Peter moved closer to her.

"I've spent years watching and waiting, biding my time and being the good boy. I thought I had my chance ten years ago with Michael, but I was wrong."

His voice trailed off, and a sad and helpless look crossed his face before his expression hardened again. Anne had no idea what he was talking about; Michael had never mentioned a friendship with Peter. In fact, he'd been rather vocal about his disdain for the boy who seemed to be the son their mother had always wanted. Quiet. Smart. Perfectly behaved.

But she wasn't about to interrupt and ask questions that might swing the pendulum of Peter's emotions to a darker, more dangerous place.

"I did whatever Marie asked of me and when she started talking about bringing you home I knew I'd have a second chance. I knew my patience would finally be rewarded. You were my ticket to becoming a real Prescott. We were always meant for each other."

Despair with a tinge of madness crossed his face, coloring his eyes a dull, flat brown.

"We would have been so perfect together…. But that isn't possible now. Marie made certain of that. She's taken the one thing I've always wanted away, so now I'm going to take what she wants most from her."

Peter slowly raised the gun until it was leveled at her chest. Anne's stomach clenched.

"I sacrificed everything so that I could be a Prescott. But I was never good enough for her. I did everything she ever asked. *Everything*. And this is how she repays me?"

His emphasis on the single word left her wondering what exactly *everything* covered. And then thinking back to what she'd just learned about her brother's death she thought maybe she didn't want to know.

And yet she couldn't stop herself from asking. "Are you the one who helped her with Michael?"

"Did I help her with Michael? No! I never would have done that to him, set him up to look weak."

Anne wasn't sure what to make of the bright gleam in his eyes until she realized it was tears. Pain and sadness looked back at her.

He'd cared about her brother.

It was a revelation that almost sent her reeling backward.

"I understood Michael." Peter stepped closer to her, his empty hand reaching out toward her. "Just like I understand you. You were both so lost and alone. Like me."

She took another halting step back, the pieces falling into place in a way that sent terror through her.

"You killed him." She hadn't meant to voice the words, realizing they would likely send him off the precarious edge of sanity, but she couldn't seem to stop herself. Something deep inside her soul needed to hear his confession to her brother's murder…even if they were the last words she ever heard.

He dropped his outstretched hand, sadness racking his body. "Yes."

Anger burst through her, hot and heavy because she could do nothing with it. Instead she asked levelly, "Why?"

His expression hardened, his grip on the gun changing

from single fisted to double. "It was an accident. He came to me that night, torn up over his conversation with your mother and your lack of sympathy."

His words were darts that nailed her right in the center of her chest.

"He'd needed a release for all that anger before he did something he'd regret. He asked me to help him. *I* was the one who was there for him that night."

"And yet you killed him. You didn't try to save him. Worse, you left him there alone."

She saw an echo of her own guilt flash across his face before he yelled, "Enough!" and took a menacing step closer to her.

He gestured for her to walk toward him. She started to shake her head, but the hardening of his face stopped her. He didn't wait for her to comply. Instead, he strode forward, grabbed her by the arm and swung them both to the opening of the path to the house.

"It shouldn't be long. I took the liberty of calling your boyfriend. He should be here any minute."

The barrel of the gun bit into her back through the thick layers of her sweater and coat. As if on cue, she saw Blake's silhouette crest a hill coming down from the house towards the line of trees.

Peter leaned in to whisper, "Right on time," and a shiver raced across her skin.

She had opened her mouth to shout at Blake—her fate was sealed but his might not be—when Peter whispered again, "I wouldn't do that if I were you. There might be a way for him to get out of this alive. If you cooperate."

Anne nodded slowly, a bead of sweat rolling down the length of her spine. How could she be warm out here in the cold?

Part of her knew he was lying. But the rest of her

hoped it was true. Either way, Blake was too close now for her warning to matter. And she knew in her heart he wouldn't have left her anyway. Not if he thought she was in danger.

"Anne?"

Blake's voice cut through the thick winter air as he approached. The temperature was dropping and her body was beginning to shake. From cold or adrenaline or fear, she wasn't sure. The sound of his voice was the best thing she'd ever heard in her life. And the worst.

Blake materialized on the dimly lit path in front of her. She fought the urge to run to him, to fling herself into his arms and let him protect her as he'd been trying to do for the past week, but she couldn't with Peter's gun pressed tight to her back.

"What's going on?" His intelligent eyes darted to the man standing behind her and she knew the moment he realized they were both in danger. His focus sharpened as his body shifted, moving his weight to the balls of his feet for better balance. She could see the glint of a gun, hidden in the folds of his winter coat. Her eyes widened and her heart collapsed in on itself.

Damn it. He was going to be a hero. The thing that made her love him the most—his selfless urge to protect—was going to get him killed. Protecting her.

She had to try to stop him. He wasn't the only one willing to sacrifice himself for the ones he loved. "Blake, why don't you go back to the house? Peter and I were just talking. I'll be right there."

She'd never know if he might have turned around and walked away, because Peter didn't give him a chance. "No, I think you should stay."

Blake's lips curled into a humorless smile as his eyes bored into the other man. Anne could feel the heat and hatred behind his stare. His gaze was a laser site, narrowed in on the man who intended to hurt her. If ever she had a doubt as to her importance to Blake, the look in his eyes right now would have taken it away. He was pissed because she mattered.

"What do you want? Why have you been terrorizing Anne?"

In that moment all pretense dissolved. Peter took a step away from her, motioning with his gun for her to move next to Blake.

"I haven't been terrorizing…. I've been nudging. Marie wanted her home. I needed her home. She was my chance to become part of the Prescott family, although that's never going to happen now. And, actually, I'm not that upset about it really. This way is going to be so much better. Marie will be gone. Annemarie will be gone. I'll be all that's left."

Anne stopped cold halfway between the two men. Peter glowered as he waved forcefully with the gun. "Keep going."

"I can't." Her legs were shaking and they absolutely refused to move another inch. She wanted to be strong in this moment, strong for Blake and for herself, but she couldn't seem to manage it.

Blake took a step toward her instead, closing the gap between them. She could feel the heat of his body and wished she could bury herself in his arms, but his nearness, at least, helped her to gather her strength. Locking her knees into place, she turned around to face Peter.

His aim was now centered directly on Blake's chest. Anne shifted her body, wanting to step between Blake and the gun, but he beat her to it. He moved a step closer to Peter, hiding her behind the wide frame of his body.

"Go ahead. You won't do it," Blake taunted.

Anne gasped. What the hell was he doing? Couldn't Blake see the hard edge of determination and madness in Peter's eyes? The man could most definitely do it.

"Blake."

"Shut up." The fact that both of them flung the words at her at the exact same moment did not sit well. The fear and adrenaline were finally beginning to fade, replaced with a healthy dose of anger. And there was plenty to go around.

"Don't underestimate me. You have no idea what I'm capable of."

Something in Blake's eyes sharpened. "Oh, but I do. You killed Michael."

"Clever, clever. Not that it's going to help you."

The look in his eyes, the focused madness, the edge of deranged pain, sent a shiver down Anne's spine. "I've found a way to have everything I've ever wanted. And have it all to myself."

Anne could see that the gun was leveled at Blake's chest. If Peter pulled the trigger now, Blake would be dead. She had to do something to prevent that. Anne walked back into Peter's line of vision, intentionally drawing his attention.

"What is it you want, Peter? I'm sure we can work something out."

When his eyes focused on her, Anne regretted her move. He was just so…unhinged. There was no hope of talking this man out of doing what he wanted. She wondered for a brief moment when his insanity had begun. When he was young and lost both of his parents? When he killed her brother in something she truly believed was an accident? When he was left alone here to bear the brunt of Marie's cold expectations? Or had it always been there and no one had noticed?

Steeling her spine, she realized it didn't matter.

"I'm so glad that you're amenable, Annemarie, because I'm going to need your help. You're going to have to die."

Blake shifted behind her, and she heard the rasp of his gun leaving its holster. While her maneuver hadn't been intended to give him cover to pull his weapon, the result was a blessing she had no intention of ignoring.

"Toss the gun away, Peter." Blake's voice was strong and commanding, serious Prescott potential. Marie would have approved.

Peter slowly turned his head back to Blake. The moment his eyes landed on the gun now pointed at his own chest, Peter threw back his head with laughter. The sound was bone chilling.

She'd heard that sometimes moments of great stress felt as if they were happening in slow motion, but she'd never experienced the sensation before today.

She could see the incremental movement of Peter's finger as he pulled the trigger. She could hear her own voice yelling out a slow warning that seemed as if it would never come in time. And she heard the report of two shots, almost as if one echoed the other.

Dark red bloomed across the front of Peter's body as he windmilled back onto the dirt path and collapsed.

Her head jerked toward Blake in time to see him fall, as well. In time to see tiny spots of blood, his blood, hang in the air as he dropped to the ground.

16

ANNE PAUSED long enough to kick Peter's gun into the dark underbrush and make sure he wasn't breathing before she ran over to Blake. She probably should have spared a moment for the other man, but just couldn't.

There was blood everywhere. It covered the front of Blake's shirt, spilling down his body so that she couldn't tell where it was actually coming from.

She slid on the pine needles and forgotten leaves as she fell to her knees beside him. "Blake? Blake? Can you hear me?"

His eyes were closed and his skin was shockingly pale. Her heart kicked inside her chest as she thought, *he's dead.*

At that moment Blake's eyes cracked open. "Is he dead?"

Involuntarily, she glanced behind her to the man who lay motionless on the ground. "Yes."

Satisfied that they were out of danger, Blake's left hand scrabbled uselessly across his body as he said, "Cell."

Anne reached into his pocket, pulling out his phone. She called 911 and the house in quick succession, yelling at George to send anyone he could to help her before throwing the cell onto the ground beside them.

Grasping Blake's coat and shirt with both hands, she ripped them apart in a desperate attempt to figure out where the river of blood was coming from.

She breathed her first small sigh of relief when she realized the bullet hole was high on his shoulder, not near his heart. Wiggling out of her coat, she wadded it up and was about to press it to his wound when his good hand reached up and stopped her.

His grip was steady and strong. "No. You'll freeze to death out here. Put that back on."

Shaking out of his hold, she muttered a prayer for fools beneath her breath and applied as much pressure to his wound as she thought he could stand.

He swore softly beneath his breath and she felt a small smile stir at her lips. Hope and relief washed through her.

"Serves you right, you idiot. Taunting him like that."

His eyes closed again and he let his head drop back down to the dirt but his lips twisted in a wry grin as he said, "This from the woman who walked between me and a madman's gun."

"Someone had to save you from yourself."

His eyes cracked open again as he looked up at her. "Saving is *my* job."

"Yeah, well, not anymore. If you ever take a bullet for me again, you won't have to worry about the recovery because I'll kill you myself."

She could hear the sirens in the distance and the pounding of several pairs of feet as help arrived. But before the chaos descended she had just enough time to hear him whisper, "Sounds fair."

THE STEADY BEEP of medical equipment greeted her as she walked into the hospital room. The scene was familiar, although it was one she really hoped they wouldn't be repeating anytime soon. She'd seen enough of this hospital to last her a lifetime. In her heart, she knew that wasn't possible, not with her mother so ill. But at the very least she could expect that Blake wouldn't be the one back in this bed.

The doctor had told her he'd be fine in several days. The bullet had gone straight through, and while it hurt like a son of a bitch—Blake's words not hers—their main concern was infection. If everything progressed nicely he'd be out in a couple of days.

Now that the immediate danger was over and there was nothing more for her to do, the echo of her terror seeped back in. She stood beside him, looking down at his slack and peaceful face, her heart once again in her throat. If she'd lost him, too…

It was something she really didn't want to think about.

"Hey." His voice was scratchy but strong as he stirred. She winced inwardly at his grimace of pain when he forgot and used his injured arm to push up higher on the bed.

Reaching for her hand, Blake pulled her gently toward the bed. For a man with a gunshot wound he was surprisingly insistent and strong. She reluctantly settled on the bed beside him—she didn't want to hurt him more.

Cupping a hand around her neck, he drew her close, resting his forehead to her own. He breathed in and his eyes closed for a moment. She could feel the kiss of his lashes as they dropped and opened again.

"I don't know what I would have done if he'd hurt

you." Pulling back, he looked straight into her eyes. "You know this means I'm never letting you out of my sight again."

She knew the words were more than they appeared on the surface. She could see the depth of his emotions churning inside his chocolate eyes. She understood them, had experienced them herself as she'd seen his blood coloring the dirt beneath his fallen body.

She never wanted to go through a moment like that again—the panic, uncertainty, fear and grief. She, as much as anyone, knew that life was uncertain. But she'd take every last second she could get with this man because each was a precious gift.

"Even if you spend every minute of the next fifty years beside me, you can't protect me from everything. Just like I couldn't protect you from that bullet."

"Even though you tried."

She smiled.

"You know what I mean. I want you in my life, Blake, but we both have lives. I'm going to be running Prescott Hotels for at least a little while and maybe for the rest of my life. You have a business of your own to run."

"Are you telling me we can't make this work?"

"No. I'm saying that neither one of us will be happy if you spend every minute we're apart worrying that someone's going to shoot at me, kidnap me…or rape me."

Blake's jaw hardened and his eyebrows lowered over his eyes. "That has noth—"

"It has everything to do with this. I might have spent the last ten years running in place, but so have you. You've built a life where your sole purpose is protecting other people. I'm ready to stop running…are you?"

She held her breath, knowing that whatever his

answer was, it would determine their fate. She wanted a future with Blake, but she didn't want one where he stood over her with one hand permanently attached to the butt of his gun.

He shifted beneath the thin white hospital sheet, his eyes drifting away from her and making her heart plummet. He wasn't ready to let the past go.

She leaned forward, protecting her heart from the blow that was coming. Instead, she was rocked back onto her rear when he looked at her. The guilt that had perpetually lurked behind his eyes was gone.

"You're right. I've known for a long time that the guilt I carried didn't really belong to me. I had no way of knowing what that guy was capable of. Karyn managed to move on. I should, too. Your brain can tell you all day long something isn't your fault…. If anyone understands how hard it is to believe, it's you."

She reached for him, crushing his mouth with her own. One of the machines behind her began to beep louder, but she didn't care. His good hand tunneled into the hair at her nape, pulling her closer.

In some small corner of her brain Anne registered that the door at her back opened and an embarrassed voice said, "Sorry," before disappearing again.

She didn't care.

Anne was the one who finally pulled back, not wanting to push Blake too far. He had lost a lot of blood. She looked down into his face, her palms rubbing against his stubble-studded cheeks. "I love you."

His eyes closed in bliss before opening again. "I love you more."

She laughed. She could see even *that* turning into a fight for control between them. But the fight would certainly be fun.

"There is one piece of bad news though."

"Oh?"

"There are hordes of reporters waiting outside. You would not believe the sensation this story has created."

His eyes closed in exhaustion but a smile touched the corners of his lips. "Just give me a couple days to recover and I'll take care of it."

She couldn't help smiling back. "Don't worry. Annemarie Prescott is pretty damn good at handling the media. Who would have thought?"

"I've always known that my Anne could do anything she wanted."

Anne left Blake to sleep and headed out into the waiting room. She was surprised to find her mother there, alone and staring silently at her feet.

Anne must have made a sound because just as she was about to leave, Marie's head shot up and their eyes connected. In that moment she couldn't have walked away even if she'd wanted to—and part of her would always want to.

"I swear I didn't know."

The pain, anguish and guilt in her mother's eyes surprised her. She never would have thought Marie had it in her.

"I'm sure other people won't understand or condone how I've lived my life—hell, I know you don't condone how I've lived my life—but I did what I had to do. There are only two things that I've ever regretted—what happened with your brother and losing you. I wanted a chance, one more chance, before I died. I didn't think that was so much to ask for."

Anne simply shook her head. "The problem, Mother,

was that you never asked. You commanded. You expected. You manipulated."

Up until that moment she'd only caught hints and glimpses of the sick woman before her. Now, she could tell that her mother was eaten up with illness.

"I realize that now. All I can say is that I thought my reasons were good ones. And that I had no idea what Peter was capable of."

That was probably as close as she'd ever get to an apology. And for both of their sakes, she was going to take it. Because in the days and weeks to come, when her mother was no longer with them, the opportunity wouldn't be there anymore.

"I believe you." It was as close as her mother was going to get to an acceptance.

Somewhere in the middle they'd find common ground for the weeks they had together. And when Marie was gone Blake would be there to help Anne through the rest.

Epilogue

"As long as we both shall live, I never want to see the inside of that hospital again."

Blake, who had turned out to be a very ornery patient, stood up from the wheelchair the nurse had insisted on and climbed into the back seat of the limo. She watched as he bumped his arm against the doorframe and winced.

"Are you sure I should be traveling?"

"The doctor said you were cleared." And there was no way she was going to take no for an answer. She'd promised his family—Karyn and his mother specifically—that they'd be home to Mississippi as soon as the doctor said he could fly. It had taken some fancy lip work from Blake to convince them not to come up to New York. They'd both wanted to insulate his family from the three-ring paparazzi circus that had camped outside the hospital.

This time, instead of going commercial, they'd be using the company jet. And as the security gate to the small private airport closed behind them, leaving a group of photogs outside the wrought iron, Anne began to appreciate the usefulness of the extravagance. Besides, in the next few months the company fleet was going to become their best friend.

Blake had offered to move his company headquarters to New York. He had clients all over the country and could really base his company anywhere. He had capable managers and was going to keep the Mississippi office open for several reasons. He didn't want to fire any of his employees who couldn't make the move and because his company had started in the South he had a large client base there. But the move would offer him new opportunities to expand more heavily into New York and D.C.

Unfortunately, it was going to be several months before the new office could open and she was needed immediately at Prescott headquarters. For a while they'd use the company jet to get back and forth to see each other as often as possible.

Anne tried not to hover as Blake moved from the car to the jet and settled into one of the plush leather chairs. He hated when she hovered.

He let out a sigh as his body sank into the wide palm of the chair.

"Are you in pain? Do you need a pill?"

He looked up at her, the ghost of a smile tugging at his lips. "No. I don't like the way they make me feel. It's manageable…I suppose." This time the grimace of pain was all show, along with the over the top sigh of suffering.

"Anything I can do?"

The glint in his eyes should have warned her. But she never would have expected a man less than an hour out of the hospital to move so quickly. Reaching out with his good arm, he snagged her around the waist and tumbled her into his lap. Even as she fell she twisted her body to make sure not to jar his injury.

"Now that you mention it..."

She couldn't help but laugh at the mischievous twist to his mouth and leering raised eyebrow. But her body heated at the sensation of his hand gliding up the inside edge of her thigh.

"The doctor did not clear you for that."

"Only because you didn't specifically ask."

"Blake." The single word was a warning. She just wondered if either of them would listen.

It had been days since the last time she'd touched him.

Underneath the pulse of need and ache of longing, there was an edge of desperation that she hoped would one day go away. Desperation to assure herself that he was alive, breathing and still hers. But even if it didn't... she'd find a way to live with it. Having Blake in her life was worth anything, including living with the fear that she might one day lose him, too. Better to enjoy the days they had.

The need inside her morphed, gentled in some ways and sharpened in others. In response, Anne laid her forehead against his and simply took a moment to breathe in the scent of him, to listen to the rise and fall of his chest and revel in the heat of him. To know that he was hers.

He growled deep in his throat as he one-armed her closer. "Now, are you going to kiss me, or do I have to get rough with you?"

"Ha! In your condition, I'd like to see you try."

Once again, his hand slipped silently up her thigh. His talented fingers found the seam of her body, even through the layers of her clothes, and rubbed. She was instantly wet, instantly aroused.

"You sure do know how to persuade a girl, don't you?"

"I'm a man on a mission. I've always wanted to join the mile high club and it seems such a waste to ignore this big empty plane."

"Oh, we'll have plenty of opportunity. We can wait." She gave him a saucy look that was the perfect blend of wanton party girl and sophisticated temptress. "Besides, the other jet has a bed."

* * * * *

HARLEQUIN *Blaze*™

COMING NEXT MONTH

Available January 25, 2011

REQUEST YOUR FREE BOOKS!

2 FREE NOVELS PLUS 2 FREE GIFTS!

HARLEQUIN®

Blaze™

Red-hot reads!

YES! Please send me 2 FREE Harlequin® Blaze™ novels and my 2 FREE gifts (gifts are worth about $10). After receiving them, if I don't wish to receive any more books, I can return the shipping statement marked "cancel." If I don't cancel, I will receive 6 brand-new novels every month and be billed just $4.24 per book in the U.S. or $4.71 per book in Canada. That's a saving of at least 15% off the cover price. It's quite a bargain. Shipping and handling is just 50¢ per book.* I understand that accepting the 2 free books and gifts places me under no obligation to buy anything. I can always return a shipment and cancel at any time. Even if I never buy another book, the two free books and gifts are mine to keep forever.

151/351 HDN E5LS

Name	(PLEASE PRINT)
Address	Apt. #
City	State/Prov.	Zip/Postal Code

Signature (if under 18, a parent or guardian must sign)

Mail to the **Harlequin Reader Service**:
IN U.S.A.: P.O. Box 1867, Buffalo, NY 14240-1867
IN CANADA: P.O. Box 609, Fort Erie, Ontario L2A 5X3

Not valid for current subscribers to Harlequin Blaze books.

**Want to try two free books from another line?
Call 1-800-873-8635 or visit www.morefreebooks.com.**

HB10R

Harlequin Romance author Donna Alward is loved for her gorgeous rancher heroes.

Meet Wyatt as he's confronted by both a precious little pink bundle left on his doorstep and his neighbor Elli who's going to show him the ropes....

Introducing
PROUD RANCHER, PRECIOUS BUNDLE

THE SQUAWKING QUIETED as Elli picked the baby up, and Wyatt turned around, trying hard to ignore the feelings of inadequacy as Darcy immediately stopped fussing.

"Maybe she's uncomfortable. What do you think, sweetheart?" Elli turned her conversation to the baby.

"What do you think is wrong?" Wyatt asked, putting the coffee pot back on the burner.

A strange look passed over Elli's face, one that looked like guilt and panic. But it was gone quickly. "I couldn't say," she replied.

"But you were so good with her this afternoon." Wyatt put his hands on his hips.

"Lucky, that's all. I just…remembered a few things." The same strange look flitted over her features once more.

Wyatt took the coffee to the table. "You fooled me. You looked like you knew exactly what you were doing." So much so that Wyatt had felt completely inept. A feeling he despised. He was used to being the one in control.

Elli and Darcy walked the length of the kitchen and back. After a few moments, she admitted, "I haven't really cared for a baby before. The things I thought of were simply things I'd heard about. Not from experience, Mr. Black."

Her chin jutted up, closing the subject but making him

want to ask the questions now pulsing through his mind. But then he remembered the old saying—*Don't look a gift horse in the mouth.* He'd benefit from whatever insight she had and be glad of it.

"I don't really know what babies need," he said. "I fed her, patted her back like you did, walked her to sleep, but every time I put her down…"

Wyatt almost groaned. Of course. He'd forgotten one important thing. He'd been so focused on getting the formula the right temperature that he'd forgotten to check her diaper. Not that he had any clue what to do there either.

Pulling calves and shoveling out stalls was far less intimidating than one tiny newborn.

"She's probably due for a diaper change, isn't she." He tried to sound nonchalant. This was a perfect opportunity. Elli must know how to change a diaper. He could simply watch her so he'd know better for the next time.

Instead, Elli came around the corner of the counter and placed Darcy back in his arms. "Here you go, Uncle Wyatt," she said lightly. "You get diaper duty. I'll fix the coffee. Cream and sugar?"

Oh boy, Wyatt thought, looking down into Darcy's pursed face, his smug plan blown to smithereens. He was in for it now.

Will sparks fly between Elli and Wyatt?

Find out in
PROUD RANCHER, PRECIOUS BUNDLE

Available February 2011 from Harlequin Romance

HREXP0211

Try these Healthy and Delicious Spring Rolls!

INGREDIENTS

2 packages rice-paper spring roll wrappers (20 wrappers)

1 cup grated carrot

¼ cup bean sprouts

1 cucumber, julienned

1 red bell pepper, without stem and seeds, julienned

4 green onions finely chopped— use only the green part

DIRECTIONS

1. Soak one rice-paper wrapper in a large bowl of hot water until softened.

2. Place a pinch each of carrots, sprouts, cucumber, bell pepper and green onion on the wrapper toward the bottom third of the rice paper.

3. Fold ends in and roll tightly to enclose filling.

4. Repeat with remaining wrappers. Chill before serving.

Find this and many more delectable recipes including the perfect dipping sauce in

NTRSERIESJAN

HARLEQUIN *Presents*

USA TODAY bestselling author

Sharon Kendrick

introduces

HIS MAJESTY'S CHILD

The king's baby of shame!

King Casimiro harbors a secret—no one in the kingdom
of Zaffirinthos knows that a devastating accident has left
his memory clouded in darkness. And Casimiro himself
cannot answer why Melissa Maguire, an enigmatic English
rose, stirs such feelings in him…. Questioning his ability
to rule, Casimiro decides he will renounce the throne.
But Melissa has news she knows will rock the palace
to its core—*Casimiro has an heir!*

Law dictates Casimiro cannot abdicate, so he must find a
way to reacquaint himself with Melissa—his new queen!

**Available from Harlequin Presents
February 2011**

www.eHarlequin.com

HP12972